WHEN WILL THEY EVER LEARN?

WHERE HAVE ALL THE GO-GO'S GONE?

Richard Baran

Where Have All The Go-Go's Gone Series™ Book 2

TotalRecall Publications, Inc.
1103 Middlecreek
Friendswood, Texas 77546
281-992-3131   281-482-5390 Fax
www.totalrecallpress.com

Copyright © 2015 by: Richard Baran
Edited by William R. "Will" Barshop
All rights reserved
ISBN: 978-1-59095-243-6
UPC: 6-43977-42430-3

Library of Congress Control Number: 2014944452
Printed in the United States of America with simultaneous printings in Australia, Canada, and United Kingdom.

FIRST EDITION
1   2   3   4   5   6   7   8   9   10

For Carol Ann—
The love of my life and girl of my dreams.

To My Daughters
Cheryl and Lisa

Author Richard Baran

holds a doctorate and two masters' degrees besides his bachelor's in business. A Navy veteran, he taught and coached for forty years at the secondary school and collegiate levels. Besides publishing a book about coaching football, this is his third novel. *The Jacket* and *Where Have All The Go-Go's Gone (Book One)* were his first two. A fourth novel, *The Dutchman's Gift* is in the printing process. He has also published a short story, *That Ain't No Walleye* and several dozen articles in professional journals. Dick and his eighth grade sweetheart, Carol, have twenty grandchildren and they divide their year between Franklin Park, Illinois; Phoenix, Arizona and Minocqua, Wisconsin.

Visit www.richardbaran.com for more information.

Acknowledgments

To my agent, Jeff Lovell for his creative right brain, impersonations of Max Bialystock (although not as good as Duke Mongan and Denny Toll) and his ability to wolf down more thin crust pizza at Chuck Romano's restaurant in Rosemont, Illinois than any three people I know.

Thanks to William Barshop for his editing prowess and the use of the term, "non sequitur." That blew me away.

My very special thanks to, Carol Ann Capuzzo Fredrickson for her convoluted inspiration and right-to-the-point comments on my writing especially, "Blah-blah-blah."

I was lucky to have several inspirational teachers who encouraged me to write. Thanks to the late, Sister Mary Helen (McBrady), B.V.M. A special thanks to Perry A. Guedry, Ph.D., and Colonel Charles Stribling of the Missouri Military Academy in Mexico, Missouri.

To: Joseph T. Baran, Chicago, Illinois, (1894-1953), Entrepreneur and Public Servant. My idol and role model. Thank you, Grandpa.

About The Book

Bo Pepperwall's intelligence dwarfed Mensa's parameters. He was perceived as strange thereby resulting in being ridiculed by many, shunned by most and being called, "Bo the Schmoe" by almost everyone. Then he faced a dilemma. He had to choose between money (which he never had) and morals (which he also lacked). He weasels a part of his recently widowed sister's inheritance for a business venture instead of turning in the killer of her husband, his despicable brother-in-law? Bo opens La Tinkerbelle's a Go-Go, a 1960's retro discotheque in an abandoned factory building in a decaying Chicago neighborhood using a theme from Peter Pan. Surrounding himself with bizarre employees (each having a unique vision of reality) who put fun into dysfunctional, his dream materializes and then nearly goes bust. Bo is saved by an egotistical, alcoholic Chicago gossip columnist who prints a story that has customers lined up at La Tinkerbelle's. Part of Bo's original dilemma gets buried in money and public adulation. Success can't cover his moral guilt and neither can a fire that destroys La Tinkerbelle's. Before he can clear the soot from his eyes, he finds himself in court charged with violations of the Mann Act, contributing to the delinquency of minors, indecent exposure, multiple business license and safety violations, ignoring Federal EPA laws, cruelty to animals and pornography. Also under arrest are members of Bo's family, important people from his prestigious suburban community Glen Forest on the Watercourse, all of his unique employees including undercover Chicago cops, the Chicago newspaper columnist and two pet cats, Heckle and Jeckle. Bo exposes the killer to the courts, is cleared of all criminal charges and finds love in the surprise ending to this screwball murder mystery.

List of Characters

General Glen Forest Pepperwall: Self-proclaimed Revolutionary War hero. He is a corrupt, conniving, lecherous coward and founder of Glen Forest on the Watercourse who fled the Battle of Savannah with his pregnant half breed girlfriend, Arvia. She later kills him while he is making love to another woman. A long line of his ancestors have kept alive the myth of his Revolutionary War heroics.

Berthold "Bo" Pepperwall: Dreamer and intellectual who was teased and picked on by his childhood playmates and carries the nickname, *Bo the Schmoe*. He is slight of build with straight, black oily hair and a pencil thin mustache that sits at a horrific angle across his lip. His appearance gives "Bag Ladies" and aging B porn stars a bad name. He is perceived by others to be a loser, misfit and social outcast enhancing his nickname. Only his sister, Arvia Pepperwall Bell, knows he is a member of Mensa and received his doctorate at age sixteen. He carries an antique Zippo cigarette lighter as a good luck charm.

Arvia Pepperwall Bell: Last female descendant of the Pepperwall name. She is a dark skinned intriguing beauty of Native American and African American blood, her black hair always worn in a single braid down her back. She abhors foul language of any kind, including slang, and has tolerated her husband's infidelities until her toleration turned into wishing he were dead.

Benoni "Ben" Bell: Intelligent, handsome, preppy son of Arvia Pepperwall Bell and Mayor Quintin Bell. His dream is to be a bass player in a rock band. He is the boyfriend of the high school librarian's daughter, Matilda and hates his father.

Quintin Bell: Another in a long line of Glen Forest on the Watercourse lecherous, conniving, corrupt mayors and the only one not of Pepperwall blood. His political fund raising parties are exhibitions of debauchery that would make Emperors Nero and Caligula salivate.

John Brown: Attorney, former college football star and best friend, on the outside, of Quintin Bell. Inside, he despises Bell and wants to see him dead. He lusts over Arvia Bell, Quintin's wife.

Matilda Newton: Seventeen year old girlfriend of Ben Bell and the daughter of Amanda Newton, the high school's librarian. Her secret dream is to be an actress. Bo Pepperwall hires her under false pretenses to her mother and father to be Tinker Bell, the star entertainment attraction in his La Tinkerbelle's a Go-Go.

Amanda Newton: High school's librarian who dreams of being the school's principal. She is the ex-wife of Sam Geronimo Germono who she hates more than sin. Next on her hate list are Quintin Bell and John Brown who, along with Alice Nell Puffin, the pastor's wife, tried to make her part of their debauchery. She mistrusts all males except Benoni Bell, and she is overly protective of her daughter.

Sam Geronimo Germono: Ex-husband of the high school librarian, Amanda Newton and father of Matilda. He left his wife for a man, a mistake that ended in tragedy. Down on his luck and a street person, he is a former saloon owner hired by Bo Pepperwall to run the beverage service at La Tinkerbelle's.

Supporting Cast

(Quirky Characters Who Put Fun in Dysfunctional)

There's a brainy spinster secretary who constantly entertains sexual fantasies about her boss; a morally loose blond bombshell and kinky wife of the local pastor who loves gin 'n tonics, saving souls and his wife—in that order. They are joined by a Police Chief who never met a Scotch he didn't like and his wife who thinks she can sing like Barbra Streisand (she doesn't) and believes she resembles the late movie star, Jayne Mansfield. She definitely doesn't. A matronly owner of a coffee house who is the drinking buddy of the mayor's secretary, two bickering gays who manage La Tinkerblle's a Go-Go's boutique, a social worker turned belly dancer dressed as a pirate and an octogenarian rock band and a hog calling champion vocalist are more quirky characters. Finally, there's a junk man who can get whatever he wants for a customer; illegal alien valet parkers dressed as pirates, the loyal head grounds keeper of the town's country club and a cantankerous judge who despises lawyers more than he does most criminals.

So: When will they ever learn?

You be the judge.

CHAPTER 1

Dreams Come True

"Be careful what you dream for," his mother had said to him almost every day of his life; at least that's how he remembered her warning; each identical statement driven home with a loving: "It might come true, Berthold."

Bo Pepperwall, loser, loner (not by choice) and known from childhood as, "Bo the Schmoe" didn't know if his dreams had come true or if he was dead. He knew dead and disappointment both started with the letter "D" and the only difference in their meanings was dead had no tomorrow. Disappointment was like the rising and setting of the sun for Bo. "Good morning, Berthold," the orange ball in the east peeking at him from Lake Michigan would say with a sly wink: "Are you ready to get dumped on today?"

Bo hadn't answered the sun in years; not since his sister had married Quintin Bell, Mayor of Glen Forest on the Watercourse who promptly moved him out of Dogwood, the gargantuan mansion of the Pepperwall estate. Bo never did get used to the small room above the massive multi-car garage that brought comfort to his brother-in-law's collection of classic cars. His room had been referred to as a coach house. The Count of

Monte Cristo had better accommodations in prison than Bo had in his drafty room. What the Count didn't have was a picture, a torn magazine cover of Bo's idol, Malcolm Forbes. Bo had discussed his daily ideas, his plans, the schemes, his finding his Treasure Island with the bold red "X" marking the spot with the magazine cover's picture as if Forbes were alive. After each discussion with his only friend outside of his sister, Arvia, Bo would leave his room eager and optimistic after he thought he heard Forbes say to him: "You're a man full of piss and vinegar, Berthold. You're eager like a beaver. You're sly as a fox. The world is your oyster. There's a brass ring with your name on it. A cigar awaits the man who can clang that bell. Now go out there and grab and clang!"

A click, not a clang, was the only thing heard; that coming from the scratched metal cover of Bo's good luck charm, his old Zippo lighter that he pilfered from his mother's bedroom dresser the day she died.

CLICK/SNAP!

Bo caressed the cap of his lucky Zippo, ran his fingers once through his oily hair and wiped the oil on his dark blue trousers that had more stains than a short order cook's apron. This was a new day. He felt more than lucky and being dumped on would never happen even if the sun guaranteed that it would.

Bo's feet bounced down the creaking, wooden back stairs of his coach house room leading to the walkway behind the garage. He felt like Fred Astaire as he headed out, exhilarated by Malcolm's locker room pep talk, to go out there and get it. Each step made him feel as if he were bouncing off a trampoline. Get it he would. No longer would he need Malcolm Forbes and his philosophies of life, liberty and the pursuit of money. There would be no need for him to call on his long time alter ego and only friend, Peter Pan for moral support. The days of his mother reading to him about Wendy, Hook and Smee were ancient history.   Peter Pan and Tinker Bell were fresh and live in his heart and soul; Peter staying with him and Bo being a special, secret member of Peter's gang. Then Bo wanted his own gang; a band of entrepreneurs more successful than Malcolm Forbes, experts all in the world of high finance and business. This day would be his day when he would shape his gang in his own image and likeness.

At the end of the day, as the sun slipped into a depressing disappearance without so much as a waving goodbye, Bo resembled an arthritic caterpillar scaling the same back stairs as if he were attempting to conquer Everest without oxygen and his Sherpa guide; Bo's backpack weighed him down with his never ending supply of D-words: Depression, degradation, disgust, deprecation and deserted by the world; but not by Peter Pan. The D's had been Bo's life fifty two weeks a year; all three hundred and sixty five agonizing days. The brass ring always seemed to be inches from his grasp, the genuine Cuban panatela waved under his nose; the CLICK/SNAP of his cherished Zippo lighter popped sparks instead of flame and one wooden milk bottle teetering on the tiny metal stand preventing him from laying claim to his Kewpie doll. He had no one to give a Kewpie doll to, but that didn't matter. Another day, another vanishing dream and then Izzy Inman's gossip column appeared in the Chicago Daily Examiner to turn all of his three hundred and sixty five depressing days into New Year's Eve, VJ Day and the Fourth of July.

Bo tried to understand the column that Sam his friend and La Tinkerbelle's a Go-Go's beverage manager and head bartender had set before him. It didn't make sense. His photographic mind wouldn't focus and he couldn't access the archives of his brain. He glanced up at Sam standing beside him, his shutter clicking overexposures, eyes asking.

Sam's answers were a series of shrugs.

Bo finished reading the column, his eyes still disbelieving; the brain of a Mensa member coughing and sputtering like an engine beyond needing a tune-up.

There was another shrug from Sam followed by a nod toward the makeshift door of Bo's office hidden in the back of La Tinkerbelle's.

He dutifully followed Sam not liking the feeling of having no feeling. He was numb but minus his backpack. Another dream, another brilliant idea to bring him fame and fortune lay crumbled at the scuffed toes of his white shoes, the laces undone. Before the worn Army surplus wool blanket Bo used as an office door could drift shut he couldn't believe the scene in front of him.   Four of his five senses had ceased working and joined numb. Depression got kicked aside by shock. He could see, but that was all, and barely. Bo was positive of one thing and that was he could inhale and exhale. What bothered him was that he couldn't feel his Zippo lighter; his security blanket that he had carried from boyhood. Peter Pan, it appeared, had also abandoned him along with Tinker Bell, Wendy, Hook, Smee and the whole gang. Even the statue of General Pepperwall on his charger rearing back in the town square of Glen Forest on the Watercourse had stopped to relieve himself.

Bo's brain coughed and sputtered as it tried to whirl in full calculating mode. His brain had started whirling about the time in his young life when he made Stanford-Binet blink at his intelligence quotient results. His mother knew her son was special after he began to recite verbatim passages she had read to him from the *Bible* and the *Encyclopedia Britannica*. She read *Peter Pan* to her son because it put him to sleep. It wasn't the story itself that put him into dreamland. He loved hugging the illustrated book's front cover. His brain continued to whirl as he passed through the threshold from child to teenager, processing and spilling out a continuous stream of ideas that baffled his mother and his older sister, Arvia. His father, Malachi, never gave any credence to what spurted out from his son and the accompanying displays of unusual, to say the least, human behavior. All he would say to his wife about his son's strange way of acting was, "He's definitely got the gene pool from your side of the family." Eventually his father packed up what he considered valuable in a gym bag, resigned his position as Mayor of Glen Forest on the Watercourse and left Dogwood, his wife and family for the arms of another woman.

The brain that wouldn't stop didn't, unable to recognize the concept of rest. Neither did memories of his mother who often said to him, "When you rest, you rust." That statement either preceded or followed her very favorite adage: "An idle mind is the Devil's workshop."

No one knew, not scientists, medical and brain doctors, even doctors with the last name of Frankenstein that Berthold Pepperwall's brain would probably keep spinning long after he had passed from his worldly life. Seeing his despicable brother-in-law murdered couldn't turn off the whirling. That whirl bothered Bo Pepperwall. He knew he had to do the right thing and report what he had seen. Doing right was, well, doing right, and Peter Pan would have done right. All Bo felt after witnessing Quintin Bell being killed was the tug-o-war dilemma of should I or shouldn't I. Bo hated dilemmas almost as much as he hated tug-o-war. He hated the game because no one wanted him on their team. None of the other kids were interested in the scientific concepts of weights, pressures and forces that Bo lectured to them like some crazed college professor. Their single response to him was, "Hang on to the end of the rope and don't let go you goddamned Schmoe." By the time Bo finished explaining to his teammates why their strategy was wrong they had lost the contest.

Dilemma was forcing Bo to choose between right and wrong. That was something he never did. He knew good and evil were different. He even knew how to choose between A-B-C-D and All of the above. He never had to make that choice. This dilemma, however, was different. This dilemma had him surrounded by people with crazed looks on their faces. This dilemma had money waving at him; the money in the hands of the same people who had the crazed looks on their faces. His brain was reaching cyclotron speeds processing data and spitting out same in business and economic terminology he could only discuss with the likes of a John Kenneth Galbraith, Milton Friedman, Keynes, Samuelson and Larry Flynt. He quickly converted the business data to a single word that all business people from corporate executives to hot dog push cart vendors understood. "Customers," he managed to mutter. That was followed in rapid fire bursts of: "Paying customers; cover charge paying customers; customers who drive cars and park in my lot." His voice grew louder with his mushrooming list of customers. "And, those customers are paying Juan and his valet parking crew twenty United States in God we trust dollars to park each of their cars." No one around him heard a word. Sam didn't. No one around him knew who he was and no one around him cared except Sam. The crowd didn't care that he was dressed in the white uniform of a cruise ship captain, his jacket buttoned on an angle, two brass buttons missing, and a large safety pin in one button hole. His hat, the black brim adorned with gold "scrambled eggs" was askance and his fly open; the bottom of his frayed, white t-shirt sticking out of the zipper opening. No one cared. Bo didn't even care. A sea of humanity clawed through the jammed open front door of his 1960's retro disco, La Tinkerbelle's like a gigantic tsunami churning up green; the green with dollar signs not related to kelp.

Death and disappointment vanished. Dilemmas were forgotten. Doing the right thing was still one of his priorities, but wasn't on the top of his list. Bo mentally shoved it on the back burner of the range in the disco's kitchen along with a kettle of lumpy mashed potatoes. Bo knew he had legs. He just couldn't feel them. He tried to walk, but couldn't. There was no sensation of his feet touching the ground. That feeling was logical because his feet weren't touching the ground. He was being pushed along by the crowd as if he were a feather propelled by a wind that had no sense of direction. Bo could make out the front entrance to his disco. At least he thought it was the front entrance. A grotesque wall of waving arms and legs punctuated with distorted faces, mouths open were attacking him from all sides. He saw their expressions of panic and heard their shouts of: "I'm-gettin'-in-here-over-your-dead-body!" screaming from those faces. Some of the crowd would spill forward and others would get caught in the back wash. His legs began to work; one white shoe made its way in front of the other white shoe; his feet, swimming in his late brother's expensive and way too big footwear, found the concrete floor of his converted World War II era steel making foundry. He recognized undercover Officer Noel Jones of the Chicago Police Department who appeared to be under siege at the front entrance. He had hired Noel initially as a bouncer and head of security. Then Noel was quickly promoted to two more jobs. He was assistant maitre d' and also personal body guard to La Tinkerbelle's star attraction, Tinker Bell. Noel faced the surging tidal wave of humanity head on from behind a gold painted maitre d' stand and red velvet rope about to be torn from its housing between two brass stanchions. Bo's shaking legs and knocking knees ceased shaking and knocking. "Hang on, Noel," he shouted. I'm coming." He didn't know Noel couldn't hear him. The person next to Bo couldn't hear him with the pandemonium. Bo, his head down, resembled a bull running the streets of Pamplona as he continued to plow in the direction of the maitre d' stand. When he got alongside Noel all he could do was stare at his security guard who stared back; both stares asking the same question: "Where did all of these people come from?"

Bo heard Noel say, "There's a ten dollar cover charge, Sir."

Then Bo saw a ten dollar bill fluttering toward the top of the stand only to be snatched from the air by Officer Jones's left hand. The ten dollar bill switched hands and ended up being dropped in a cardboard whiskey carton that Noel had gotten from one of Sam's bartenders, another Chicago cop moonlighting for Berthold Bo Pepperwall. The cash in the whiskey carton had piled up into a mountain spilling out of the box in the few minutes since Bo had joined Noel. The police officer was perspiring as if he had chased a drug dealer from the Oak Street Beach west to the nearest suburban town in late August. He was a blur of hands and arms collecting money as fast as he could. It didn't matter to him that the money was missing the cardboard carton and collecting on the floor.

It didn't matter either to Bo. He blinked, caught his breath, regained his composure and said to the nearest fist clenching money: "Welcome to La Tinkerbelle's. There's a ten dollar cover charge." The word, charge had barely cleared his mouth and he found himself being bombarded by money that was being tossed at him from all angles. "Thank you," he kept repeating as he stuffed bills in all denominations into his soiled white trouser pockets, the pockets bulging in a matter of minutes.

Money made sense to Bo. His family always had money, lots of it even if he never had a dime. Mayhem, however, was a concept that was foreign to him. Bo believed in orderly chaos, another of the many chapters in the story of his life. He was always responsible for the chaos and order somehow followed, although in a helter-skelter fashion that only he understood. Since his brother-in-law, Mayor Quintin Bell, was found dead on the Glen Forest on the Watercourse croquet course lawn at his annual political fund raiser, Bo's life had turned into a chaos that confused him. Seeing a croquet mallet crush in the side of his brother-in-law's head not once, but three times was enough to almost bring religion into Bo Pepperwall's life. Religion, however, did not have the power of money. It didn't have the power of a wooden croquet mallet pulverizing human bone. Opportunity had that power and Bo, muscles flexed, had jammed his own mallet into an opening he knew would bring him wealth and prestige along Chicago's North Shore. Here was his chance.

Bo's chance, like the daily greeting from the morning sun, saw him as the dumpee, the recipient of ridicule, his dream being bashed against the rocks of a Lake Michigan breakwater like so many angry waves trying to pull Bo out into the depths of the lake when he discovered he was left out of his brother-in-law's will. He popped up to the lake's surface, gasping, a new plan on his drawing board, this one to convince his sister, Arvia, Quintin's widow, to take a portion of her estate and invest in an idea he had for her. His plan didn't take into account his almost choking to death when he swallowed a chunk of a Chicago style hot dog that resembled something Friar Tuck would have torn from a leg of mutton. His sister didn't approve of his manners or eating habits, but she felt a desire to enlarge her world, to escape from Dogwood and being more than a Pepperwall. She surprised herself and her brother by saying to him, his mouth and lips still smeared with the yellow mustard and green pickle relish that hadn't found his trousers: "I like your idea, Berthold. I think having a small business venture, something like dabbling in a trendy Gold Coast boutique, would provide me with a diversion to all of this." Her plastic floral glass of iced tea made a slow, sweeping pass across the grounds of her estate, the mansion, the only home she had ever known, acting as a backdrop.

Bo couldn't believe his sister had agreed to go along with his idea for financing his idea of a business venture. He didn't tell his sister that his idea for her would eventually become, La Tinkerbelle's a Go-Go, a discotheque in the heart of a Chicago slum area. His rationalized plan was crafted by him exclusively for her; an idea to provide her with a source of social activities while she adjusted to her new role as grieving widow. His sister neither grieved nor needed adjustment. She didn't need the financial gains her brother had predicted she would garner. Her brother did. Any money would increase his wealth. Even a penny added to his lint filled pockets was more than he had now. He didn't know why he had used the expression, grieving widow as part of his rationale to sell his idea to her. His sister despised her husband and often wished he would go away like their father had left their mother. Getting killed by a croquet mallet wasn't a part of her wishes although it worked. As for Bo, all he wanted was a monetary crumb or two for providing his creative options and handle the financial affairs that would compensate him for his efforts. His plans also toyed with taking his few crumbs and turning them into a full loaf; perhaps an entire bakery. He remembered his mother reading a story to him about some guy who took a loaf of bread and a fish and parlayed those into a market day of some kind.

Bo understood that sooner or later he would have to report the killer of his brother-in-law to the authorities even if it meant giving up the opportunity to help his sister and himself to financial gain. Peter Pan, he knew, would have done the same thing.   Bo's Mensa qualifying brain was not accustomed to designing morally correct options.   Morals, scruples and ethics were never options he faced.   He knew he wasn't alone.   Most politicians had the same beliefs.   Like politicians, he was not accustomed to necessarily doing the right thing.   Now he had no such concerns.   His sister had taken care of such things by stating three simple words: "I like it."

He had stuttered, stammered, gasped, coughed, choked and stopped breathing before he could finally say to Arvia, "Sis, you really like what I've planned for you?"

His sister had nodded then added a reassuring smile that she wasn't teasing him like an older sister once taunted her younger brother.   So many times before he thought he was spinning at the end of a string in a yo-yo youth contest where he rocked the cradle or went round the world only to have his string break.   His sister liked his idea.   Not only did she like it, she was going to finance it.

Bo continued to hold his ground, braced shoulder-to-shoulder alongside of Noel Jones, all senses now operating at maximum efficiency.   He not only saw the throng of paying customers all but rioting to gain entrance to La Tinkerbelle's a Go-Go, he saw their money.   For the first time since his business venture had come to fruition he saw the disco's flashing lights; heard the loud period music from his octogenarian band of

Regis, Reggie and Rommie and saw white knee high boots belonging to leggy dancers in scant costumes in his hanging cages. Most of all, Bo's senses sniffed and tasted money. He smelled that money. He even ran the tip of his tongue over Jackson and Jefferson; almost choking on Ulysses. He looked at the blur of Noel Jones and asked: "Are the guys here?"

"Guys," repeated Noel without taking his eyes off the currency being thrust at him.

"Guys," echoed Bo. "You know, Tinker, Peter and Pan. Are they here? Are they ready to perform?

Noel still tossed money under the maitre d' stand while sweat poured off of him. "I think Cubbie and Davia are here," he said, sounding out of breath. "I thought I saw them come through the fire exit door by your office."

"Cubbie and Davia?" asked Bo.

"Yeah," said Noel. "You know, Peter and Pan." He gave Bo a quizzical look. "You do know the real names of your employees, don't you?"

"Oh," muttered Bo. "Oh, yeah, Peter and Pan." He blinked then asked, "But what about Tinker?"

Noel shrugged. "I haven't seen Matilda at all."

"Our star attraction isn't here?" Bo said, feeling his senses were about to abandon him again.

"Maybe you better call her, Mr. Pepperwall," said Noel Jones, his efficiency purring along. His left hand snatched money while his right hand would snap open the brass clip securing one end of the velvet rope. Several happy eager customers rushed by him looking as if they had just entered the Eighth Wonder of the World. Then the brass clip snapped shut.

"Call her," said Bo sounding out of breath. "Yeah, call her.

That's what I'll do." He glanced at Noel. "Take the helm, Noel," he ordered. "Steady as she goes. There's no wave in this here ocean that can bring down the Jolly Roger and La Tinkerbelle's. Call her. That's what I've got to do."

CHAPTER 2

Common Sense

The sixth sense, the one that turned Bo into a schmoe, the one that heaped ridicule on him all of his life, the one that popped his daily balloons and kept the rising morning sun eager to greet him, jumped up like a macabre Jack-in-the-box yelling, "Boo, Bo!" The sixth sense let out a Stephen King laugh. Then, stating nonchalantly: "Here I am like always, Bo." His jester's hat bells jingled and he grinned. "It's me, your buddy, Jack, and I'm ready to help you make an ass out of yourself again?"

The morning sun's circle seemed to shake slowly from side-to-side as it said: "If you intend to join the ranks of dumpers like yours truly, put on your silly hat, wipe that befuddled look off your face and get ready to rumble."

Bo heard of common sense. His mother had often said to him as he was growing up: "Berthold, you don't have a lick of common sense in that wonderful brain of yours."

"Sure I do, Mom," he'd reply politely. "I don't know why you always say that."

When his mother was on her death bed her last words to her son were, "Think, Berthold." She let out a sigh. "Try to have your brain engaged before you move your tongue."

Bo finally did think, but that was after countless balloons

had gone pop almost making him go deaf and being a target for his brother-in-law's venom. Then Quintin Bell was dead and Bo was resuscitating a long ago abandoned steel foundry, turning it into a 1960's retro discotheque. With his creation came a loud click from within his skull. His brain was engaged and his Zippo sent out the congratulatory announcement.

CLICK/SNAP!

His initial application of his mother's last wish for him was to hire Sam Geronimo Germono to be his Director of Beverage Services and his head bartender. With Sam came his two pet black cats, Heckle and Jeckle. To Bo, Sam's pets were a nuisance and he couldn't figure out how an adult, a male especially, could talk to a couple of fury four-legged animals as if they were human. "Do they really understand what you're saying to them?" he had asked Sam.

"I guess," said Sam. "Doesn't make any difference," he continued. "They're a lot smarter than most people I know."

"They're cats," remarked Bo, his reply filled with frustration because Sam gave his pets more attention than he gave to Bo. His oft neglected intuition also came into play when he employed three females. Two of the females were in their early to mid-twenties and taught kindergarten in a Jewish synagogue elementary school. Bo advertised and promoted them as Peter and Pan. His third female hire was unique. She was daughter of Sam Geronimo. Her uniqueness entered Bo's life when her father threatened to dismember Bo if, as Sam so succinctly stated: "If so much as one hair on my little girl's hair gets harmed in your lame brain scheme, you're going to have to get your cop buddy, Officer Jones to get a body bag from the coroner's office for your remains."

Sam's daughter, unbeknownst to her father, was destined in Bo's mind to be La Tinkerbelle's star attraction. Bo billed her as Tinker Bell; her name flashing from a marquee Bo had bought from his supplier and friend, John Cinderella. Matilda Newton was Sam's daughter. She also had a mother. And, her mother was the Glen Forest on the Watercourse high school's librarian and Sam's ex-wife, Amanda who detested Sam Geronimo Germono.

The only physical trait that Matilda had in common with her east coast, once socialite mother was that, like her mother, she was well endowed. Matilda was a senior and classmate of Ben Bell, Bo's nephew. She was also his girl friend.

Bo, his creative genius knowing no bounds and usually lacking anything resembling good taste, had his unique trio of young ladies swing across the discotheque's ceiling suspended by wires and special harnesses. They would soar back and forth above six cages, each with a go-go dancer. The dancers never saw the trio and the trio only saw the tops of the cages.

Bo's brain wasn't totally in synch with his tongue when he shocked his sister by hiring a gay odd couple, Franco and Charles, to run the discotheque's boutique. To his sister and all of the residents of the prestiege community of Glen Forest on the Watercourse, gay meant happy and carefree. He gave himself another pat on the back and double clutched his tongue when he hired an octogenarian band, who he dubbed Cap'n's Kids. He added an Arkansas hog calling champion, Obadiah Ledbetter, to be the band's vocalist. He came accompanied by his common law wife, Emerine who appeared old enough to be his grandmother. Bo was pure, bottom line business when he decided to go into partnership with the Chicago Police officers he met who were patrolling the neighborhood around his purchase of the abandoned foundry. The cops jumped at the idea of providing security while moonlighting as waiters, waitresses and bartenders. They bought into Bo's idea of being dressed as pirates because most of them were undercover. The main reason for their jumping at Bo's offer was of the financial compensation package Bo offered. They would each become a part owner of La Tinkerbelle's. The more money the disco made, the more they would make. Besides, all of their tips would be split between the owners equally. Bo included himself in the split.

Bo didn't totally trust the police. He couldn't watch everyone and be everywhere so he hired the gatekeeper to the Dogwood estate to be his eyes and ears at La Tinkerbelle's. Hans, who wore a uniform identical to the German Brown Shirts—minus the swastika—came complete with his two German Sheppard guard dogs, Schickle and Gruber. Bo also made sure Hans was minus his Hiel, Hitler salute.

His late mother's warning about brain and tongue synchronization was put to the test when Bo stuck his foot, up to the ankle, in his mouth and momentarily returned to being Bo the Schmoe. He couldn't figure out why all of his new employees looked at him in disbelief when he also hired Obadiah's common law wife, Emerine Randall to join the band as a tambourine player. "After all," Bo said to Sam, "tambourines were big in the sixties."

Sam's two pet cats disagreed with Bo's decision, scampering away as fast as possible when Emerine came into view.

Bo was still standing next to Noel at the maitre d' stand; money, soft, floating non-clinking money, being plucked from the air by two sets of hands. What wasn't plucked and transferred into the whiskey carton under the stand fell gently to the floor where two sets of feet did a spastic dance shuffle making sure the money was somewhat hidden under the gold painted stand with the jolly roger symbol on the front; the words: *Welcome to La Tinkerbelle's* stenciled across the front. Under the welcome message were the words: *Quarters Available for the Men's Room.*

"You'd better call Matilda, Bo," said Noel, his eyes scanning the crowd inching through the main entrance as if he were on a stake-out. "I can steer your ship through this squall. You can count on me."

Bo blinked as he continued to stuff money into his uniform pockets as if he were a robot set on high speed. He muttered, "I should call her." He blinked again. "Yeah, right, call her. I need my star attraction," he said to Noel who didn't hear him. "Call her," he continued in a subdued voice. "That's what I'll do, I'll call Matilda." His blink rate increased and he could hear his mother's words. "Right, Mom, common sense. Of course, I have common sense," he answered back to her as he turned and saw wall-to-wall and shoulder-to-shoulder people. They all held a drink glass; some had a drink glass in each hand. "It's finally happened, Malcolm," he blurted out as his eyes began to water, his mind whirling. "Noel's right, Malcolm, I've got to call her," he murmured, pushing himself into the crowd. "Oh, dear God, look at all these people. Look at all these customers. Look at all this money. It's really happening, Malcolm." He stopped, turned and could barely see Noel at the maitre d' stand. His ship was on course. "Steady as she goes, Noel," he yelled. No one heard him, his order being swallowed up by a nasty nor'easter of deafening shouts. He turned back to continue into the crowd and make his way to his tiny office made up of stacks of wooden pallets set in a eight by eight square eight feet high. The inspiration, founder, designer, builder and soon-to-be tycoon needed the privacy of his office for one of the most important phone calls of his life. "Ice," he muttered. "We can't run out of ice. We must fill up those thick bottomed glasses with lots of ice. Liquor costs dollars; ice costs pennies. Bottom line, Berthold; never forget the bottom line. Americans doing business in China don't. Malcolm, you sly dog, you never did."

The crowd noise was beyond deafening. Bo pushed and shoved then he shoved and pushed. For every push and shove forward he got pushed and shoved back. He started saying, "Excuse me. Excuse me." But no one listened. They were too busy pushing and shoving to get a better view of the bandstand. Frustrated at being ignored in his efforts to be polite and get to his office, Bo decided to take matters into his own hands.

Yelling, FIRE he did not. Shouting, "Move it or lose it. You'll look funny without it," never happened making his mother extremely happy, if only for a moment, as she looked down on her successful son. Then she cringed and said, "Oh, Judas priest, Berthold," as she watched her son drop both his hands to his side. Before a patron on each side of him realized they had been goosed and who did the goosing, Bo was well into cutting a path toward his office. He surged ahead his whirling mind repeating one word to him. "Dilemma-dilemma-dilemma," he heard. "I know, I know, I know," he answered. "Mom, I'll do the right thing. I'll do the right thing. I promise, Mom."

His mother's eyes were shut and her hands covered her ears.

Bo's hands ached but he kept groping; pinching, poking, prodding and goosing; opening up a path to his office that was now in sight. He stood on his toes for a minute and looked to his right. The boutique was packed. He could see a sea of hands like a school of octopi clutching every item that had been on display in the boutique. The clothing waved like a parade of military flags on amphetamines. Franco was at the cash register. He didn't see Charles, but knew he was there by the way heads in a certain area of the boutique seemed to bob up and down, astonished looks on those faces. A quick glance to Bo's left made his heart race. The entrance to the men's room was jammed, the door forced open. "Oh, do keep inserting quarters into those inviting slots," he stated. Several more gropes had him inches from his office door blanket. "Call her," he repeated again and again. "Get her down here now." He slid into his office the Army surplus blanket he had bought from John Cinderella at John's Junk Store covering the entry. "Have her take a cab or a limo; charter a darned old helicopter."

He thought, made a face and said to his office. "That'll cost too much money. Bottom line, Berthold; think bottom line." He felt the bulges of money in his uniform pockets and reached for the phone.

His mother's face was now buried in her hands. He didn't hear her choked warning.

CHAPTER 3

<u>Revenge</u>

Amanda Newton embraced the privacy of her high school library office as if she were in the arms of an imaginary lover. There had been no lovers in her life since her divorce from Sam Geronimo Germono, only a fantasy that ended in disaster, teaching her a lesson about winning and losing. She learned what happens when a sweet, secret yearning gets squashed by a trio of sour lemons. The only love she now felt was for her daughter, Matilda, and the comfort she savored being surrounded by shelves of books. Each book she called her friend, dispensing a hug, a loving embrace given only to those deemed worthy of her affection. The librarian's pleasures were simple. A morning cup of a hazelnut-cinnamon blended coffee laced with a powdered French vanilla creamer eased her into the start of each work day. Saturday she enjoyed the luxury of an additional hour of sleep, Sunday was reserved for a brunch she prepared for her and her daughter after they returned from a Mass in Latin at Saint John Cantius Catholic Church in Chicago. Amanda loved Latin and she was going to be sure that her daughter would harbor that same love. "Do all you can to keep this beautiful classic language alive," she had said to Matilda so many times until her daughter started repeating in the privacy of her tiny bedroom a poem she had seen scribbled on the inside cover of an old Latin text book headed for the incinerator. *Latin is a dead language. Dead as dead can be. It almost killed the Romans and now it's killing me.*

The aroma from Amanda's coffee inched her into a state of mild intoxication, a strange feeling for a Monday. School was closed for a local holiday, this one honoring the town founder, General Glen Forest Pepperwall. She kept her coffee warm in an insulated mug embossed with a black line depiction of Charles Dickens, his words reminding her: "It was the best of times; it was the worst of times." The librarian submersed herself slowly into in what she called, *MT*, her abbreviation for My Time.

Nothing in the school's library indicated that a founder of Glen Forest on the Watercourse ever existed. Even the high school's principal, Melvin "Overcoats" White had no memory of General Glen Forest Pepperwall's history. Then, again, Principal White, his senility advancing faster than the town's founder retreating from harm's way or the late Mayor Quintin Bell scurrying off with a female for his perverted idea of sampling candy and a co-ed steam bath, was in a daily state of confusion. Melvin White's senility had slowly spread from forgetting to zip up to catching himself sometimes not zipping down. Then zipping didn't matter after the principal was found dead the same night and at the same place as Mayor Bell. Actually, he was found the next morning by Rip Repeater and his Glen Forest on the Watercourse Country Club ground crew. Melvin White appeared to be sound asleep in one of the high back dining room chairs that had failed to make the water hazard at the Mayor's fund raising party. No mention was ever made that his trousers were down around his ankles and traces of lipstick visible from his waist to his knee caps. Rip gave a knowing smile; his crew sported broad grins, but only for a moment. For them, the morning after a Mayor Bell hosted party at the Glen Forest on the Watercourse Country Club was business as usual; monkey business as they viewed the clean up. This was the first time they cleaned up after a death; two deaths to be precise.

Founder's Day, regardless of who founded what and on what day, was a holiday and belonged to Amanda Newton. Her life, she felt, had been in turmoil, a ball of yarn attacked by a room full of playful kittens. There was no sign of playful in her life. Everything she had ever wanted had been taken from her. Everything, that is, except her most cherished possession, her daughter. Amanda Newton once summed up her philosophy of life in one capitalized word, D-I-G-N-I-T-Y. That was before dignity took a dive and her husband left her for another, that other a man. That initial jolt sent her spinning out of control worse than Alice discovering the real Wonderland. Her contorted spin continued on a downward spiral for years, her ugly journey seeing her dignity damned along with almost anything and everything associated with her existence. Then, as if by a miracle, by Divine intervention, a chance to enter a real wonderland appeared. Mayor Quintin Bell invited her to one of his country club social functions, the invitation hinting at her being considered to be the next principal of the Glen Forest on the Watercourse High School, a much coveted dream of hers.

Amanda primped, preened and prepared for the evening which she felt would restore dignity to her life. Class, manners, appropriate behavior and a return to the social graces was what she envisioned. Why wouldn't she believe her life was about to take a turn for the best? She was being escorted by Mayor Quintin Bell into an envied circle of the who's who of society along Chicago's prestigious North Shore. She was being considered to replace Melvin White in a job that she had been doing for years; Principal White only able to read announcements over the school's P.A. system when he could remember and when he could find the microphone; that, with Amanda's tender guidance.

Amanda Newton had entered the Glen Forest on the Watercourse Country Club looking, feeling and acting like Cinderella going to the ball. She left barefoot, her dress torn, bra missing and hair disheveled. Her pumpkin never had the chance to become a golden, horse drawn carriage. It was squashed under Alice Nell Puffin's stiletto heels. What wasn't squashed met a croquet mallet. Amanda Newton limped home on a cut and swollen foot vowing, in not so lady like language, that somehow she would get revenge on Mayor Quintin, John Brown and Pastor Puffin's wife. Her nightmare was later put to rest several years later when she heard of the Mayor's death. Actually, she heard the sound of his death; a croquet mallet making contact with the Mayor's skull. To be exact and factual, she heard the mallet's contact three times because she was there; a party crasher and witness.

Amanda Newton had violated her own strict code of social behavior and attended the Mayor's party without a formal invitation. In other words, she crashed it. In one hand she held her letter of resignation. Her other hand clutched a one quart plastic container marked Circle K filled to the brim with her favorite, George Dickel Tennessee sour mash and Seven Up mixed half and half. Her need to walk in unannounced at the

Mayor's latest party was heightened by the news she had heard that Lucia Gunderson, the former Head Mistress of the Glen Forest Country Day School and rumored paramour of Mayor Bell, had replaced Melvin White as principal. The next morning after crashing the Mayor's party and witnessing what turned out to be his death, she discovered that Melvin was also found dead the morning after the party.

Quintin Bell's demise triggered a spring board of events that included the Mayor's son, Benoni, spending an inordinate amount of time with the librarian's daughter, Matilda. Amanda's woman's intuition and motherly instincts told her something wasn't right. Intuition and instincts couldn't have been more correct.

MT, her flavored coffee and the peace and quiet of her library office helped keep Amanda Newton's chin propped up. Today belonged to her. She had the entire school to herself free of adolescent pandemonium; free, she hoped, of Lucia Gunderson who she detested even more since Lucia was now her new boss. Amanda, somehow, still harbored the belief that one day she would be the principal of the Glen Forest on the Watercourse High School Slashing Rapiers.

Amanda Newton needed MT, needed it more than anything in her life. Amanda Newton's reasons for MT were many and varied, each tied to her hatred for the late Mayor, his attorney friend, the lecherous John Brown and Pastor Rufus Puffin's adulterous wife, Alice Nell. There were more residents of note in Glen Forest on the Watercourse she had no use for. Included on her extensive list and in no particular order of importance, were Linda Ann Finn the police chief's anorexic wife who sported artificial boobs, the size more than ample enough for at least three females in need. The police chief's wife also thought she looked like the late movie star and sex symbol, Jane Mansfield—she did not, and could sing like Barbra Streisand— she could not. Amanda also detested Rodney "Bird Dog" Pointer, President of the School Board because she felt he had sold her out at Mayor Bell's urging. She was right.   She felt embarrassed that she had wished John Brown, Alice Nell Puffin and Lucia Gunderson would have joined Mayor Bell in death. Death had always been too vile of a word for her to wish on any human being, even her ex-husband, although he didn't deserve to live either.

There were other town residents who didn't meet Amanda Newton's criteria of possessing all of her social redeeming values.   Nevertheless she tolerated each.   Wanda Mensch, Mayor Bell's efficient and loyal secretary lived in the same building as did Amanda. They had the two apartments located above Shake's Mortuary on one side of the town square. The extent of her association with Wanda Mensch was the exchanging of pleasantries in the evening when each would return from work. The pleasantries were limited to a cordial, polite, but somewhat chilled, "Good evening" and those exchanged, at best, once or twice a week.   Not as close by, but still a neighbor of sorts, was Mildred Farnsworth Pepperwall Jones, proprietor of the coffee shop, Mildred's Ennui Latte' Emporium, located directly across from Shake's Mortuary. Amanda had heard that Mildred was related to one of the founders of the Daughters of the American Revolution and was the sister of a judge. She had heard it was the Supreme Court, but was dubious. Mildred's advanced years, her DAR lineage and family blood linked somewhere on the chain of the judicial system allowed Amanda to enter the coffee shop. That was only once after she discovered what Mildred Farnsworth Pepperwall Jones charged for a cup of flavored coffee. "Not on my librarian's salary," she had muttered, glancing at the menu prices on a sign behind the counter. She quickly left the emporium.

No one on the staff at Glen Forest on the Watercourse High School had dedicated herself more to the school or her job than did Amanda Newton. Her library was award winning, garnering a plethora of plagues, trophies and framed certificates that the librarian displayed throughout her domain like an interior designer's layout in *Architectural Digest*. "For you, my friends," she said to the shelves of books throughout the library. "Share with me, please." The librarian loved teaching and guiding students to enjoy reading. She thrilled at showing them what a vast, beautiful and glorious world was available to them in the form of the written word if only they would put their thumbs to rest and bury the newest and up-to-date versions of cellular phones and texting. Her greatest love, however, outside of her daughter, was a desire she clasped firmly to her heart and perfectly shaped bosom to be the principal of Glen Forest on the Watercourse High School. Rumors had been around for at least ten years that the elderly principal, Melvin "Overcoats" White, was close to retiring or expiring. Other rumors had him as the first and only principal the school ever had. At least it appeared that way. Amanda tried not to get involved with rumors. She dealt strictly with factual data. Then the fact that Lucia Gunderson had literally screwed her way into the job that Amanda desired sent the librarian's emotions into a state of turmoil that resembled something going on in Bo Pepperwall's head.

Melvin White was a company man who wore his belted, plaid, flannel lined, London Fog trench coat daily from the start of school after Labor Day to graduation the Memorial Day weekend. Jokes and innuendos flourished about the trench coat. Melvin White appeared not to notice, not to hear, counting the days to when he would really retire and spend the rest of his life in a climate warm and sunny laced with tropical breezes and a never ending supply of Mai-Tai's. One thing that didn't go unnoticed was the fact that Melvin White never missed a day of school because of illness. What did go unnoticed was that no one, not one public official, C.P.A., lawyer or anyone else possessing fiscal knowledge ever bothered to check the principal's annual budget and related expenditures. Where many thought the principal's mind could have used its own trench coat, he carefully concealed, over time, a retirement nest egg that would enable him to own a villa somewhere in the Caribbean where he could also afford to own the distillery that produced the rum that made his Mai-Tai's. He couldn't wait for the day when he would be known as Mel the Beachcomber.

It was Amanda Newton who directed the activities of Glen Forest on the Watercourse High School from behind the scenes when the principal began to, as some astute faculty members stated, "Lose his marbles." Amanda oversaw the directives, the state mandates, the federal guidelines, but never the budget. She guided Principal White's hand; pen firmly clasped in it, across many a dotted line. Her whispered words had him stating what had to be stated over the school's P.A. system. Sometimes her shoulder received Melvin's frustrated tears, his nose running, her blouse or sweater or blazer blotting up same. She had no idea that he kept funneling money into a secret account just as she had no idea that Lucia Gunderson, with unwanted assistance from Alice Nell Puffin, caused other parts of Melvin White to be blotted up.

The shocking news that Melvin White's body had been discovered after the Coroner's Office had carted off the Mayor's remains was the second insult endured by Amanda Newton at the hands of Quintin Bell. She never knew of the Coroner finding lipstick traces on Melvin White's remains. No one did except Rip Repeater and his grinning crew. The Coroner discretely left off traces of cosmetics from his official report out of respect for Melvin who had been his biology teacher at the high school four decades earlier. "Melvin, you sly, old sumbitch," muttered an envious Coroner Mac McDuffy. Mac, as a student, had been caught by Melvin White as Mac and cheerleader captain, Gretchen Goodspeed were engaged in the first hand learning of the human anatomy in the biology lab. Melvin, after muttering a loud, "humph" had turned and left the started teenagers without saying a word. Nothing was ever said of the incident and Mac, eventually forgetting Gretchen's charms and athletic nimble physique, never forgot Melvin White. The only mention of lipstick traces on Mac's report had been absorbed by the four walls of his office.

Rumors weren't as kind as Mac's report. The dished dirt spread like a swarm of hungry locusts devouring a grassy African plain. The first rumor was true. Melvin White had been seen with Amanda Newton crying on his shoulder and then her leaving in a huff, someone recalling her saying, "You sold me out for that vile vibrating vagina from Virginia." That rumor was before the Mayor's fatal party. The next rumor, and apparent last sighting of Melvin White alive, was spread by Linda Ann Finn. The police chief's wife swore she witnessed an unsteady principal being escorted by Lucia Gunderson and Alice Nell Puffin past the eighteenth green water hazard on his way to what she thought was the parking lot. The word, unsteady in Linda Ann Finn's statement made complete sense to all who heard it. A man Melvin White's age couldn't handle the likes of either Alice Nell or Lucia on his best prescription filled day. Sandwiched in between the two of them was what fantasies were made of, that, and massive heart attacks.

Amanda Newton knew that before Mayor Bell died he by-passed his own National Search Committee of learned academicians, business heavyweights and several state representatives to literally give Lucia Gunderson a boost directly to the principal's office at the high school. Lucia Gunderson, before the announcement of her appointment was made public, had her new office transformed into a brighter, bolder, even bawdier Victorian den of inequity than her Country Day School office where Mayor Bell once rearranged her furniture—with her on it.

Before Amanda Newton could provide proof of the improprieties–she owned her own new cell phone with picture taking qualities–Quintin Bell and Melvin White were dead.

Amanda Newton was not one for imbibing. After Lucia Gunderson became principal, a countless number of high balls made with George Dickel Tennessee Sour Mash and Seven Up became a part of the librarian's diet. It was a drink she remembered her mother inhaling upon learning her husband was having a sordid affair with the local all-girl prep school's lady's field hockey coach. Amanda couldn't numb the pain of her loss nor, as she found, drink the distillery in Tennessee out of inventory. She did get them to put on a third shift.

Amanda sat perched on her padded, high back stool that was rumored to have once been part of the décor of the world famous Chez Paree in downtown Chicago. Her stool had been a gift, an apology of sorts, from Mayor Quintin Bell. She had wanted, Hal, the frail, ghost like custodian who kept the school's library carpeted floors vacuumed to hospital operating room cleanliness, to toss the chair into one of a dozen trash dumpsters behind the school. Her mind reconsidered once her bottom felt the genuine leather cushion giving her a caress she would never slap at the way she had slapped and kicked at Quintin Bell. Many nights following that heinous encounter found her entertaining thoughts of what turned out be a masquerade ball, the masks not as ugly as the faces behind them. On a rare lonely moment in her back room library office, there was Dickens stating to her about the best and worst of times then adding a twisted touch of Shakespeare with a wink, "To kill or not to kill? That is the question." She recalled seeing a paperback during that incident, the book being found in Melvin White's office and destined for the garbage. The book was Mickey Spillane's, *I the Jury*. The author had winked at her, perhaps it had been Mike Hammer; she wasn't sure. She was sure at what was said to her, a second wink thrown in for effect, "You wanted that slimy bastard dead didn't you, Baby. Fess up. A guy like me never rats on a gorgeous dame with gams like yours." Mike Hammer made the librarian shiver as she read every page. Mickey Spillane became one of her favorite authors.

Amanda, after hours of rationalizing, allowed herself to return to the scene of the crimes perpetrated against her by Quintin Bell, John Brown and Alice Nell Puffin. Her intent was to resign as librarian, take her daughter, Matilda and move back home to the eastern seaboard. Yes, she had crashed the Mayor's political fund raiser. Yes, she had too much Dickel and Seven. Yes, she fell face first into the eighteenth green's sand bunker after witnessing wood collide with bone three times. Dickel and Seven enhanced her memories of Alice Nell Puffin, a bare breasted police chief's wife screeching out her rendition of, "Happy Days are Here Again" and a belly dancer named Naomi. She couldn't erase the loud metallic sounding clicks and snaps she heard that night. Those metallic clicks along with the sound of a croquet mallet slamming into Quintin Bell's head had abruptly sent her to contingency Plan B after Plan A had been derailed before she could get the mayor to reconsider his appointment of Lucia Gunderson to the job that he had all but promised to her. She was not proud of her original plan, one that had her braless and justifying that the worst of times necessitated drastic actions. She was embarrassed by what she would do to become principal. Amanda, brazenly strolling into the Mayor's party after hiding her empty Circle K cup in the branches of an arborvitae for a later retrieval, was surprised that no one gave her a questioning look. She had fortified herself with additional liquid courage guzzling four assorted cocktails, two of them full shots of tequila. She had taken the drinks from a tray left on a table by Bo Pepperwall who was working as, among other things, a bus boy. The drinks joined George Dickel in her empty stomach and she found herself disoriented, dizzy and losing her sense of direction. She finally ended up face down in a corner of one of the eighteenth green's circle of vast sand bunkers. The sand and the affects of the alcohol seemed to drive away her desire to use her body to buy the principal's position.   Had she known of her daughter's secret joke with Benoni Bell, the two fingered *V* sign representing the librarian's late book fine, "Two cents, please," she would have needed a third plan.   That plan, however, had no way of being implemented.   At that point, the librarian wouldn't have been able to utilize all of her fingers and toes.   She couldn't find them.   Sprawled out in the sand, she abandoned prostituting herself when she realized Quintin Bell didn't care that she was a Vassar graduate and woman of letters.   Her Phi Beta Kappa status meant zero to him.   His college days saw him belonging to such jocular Greek organizations as, Rape Adame Aday, I Felt a Thigh and Tapa Keg Anight.   Brushing sand off her face and spitting it from her mouth, Amanda Newton vowed she would no longer try to drive away her misery the same way her mother had tried.   Her vow wouldn't be easy as she curled up in the sand craving the sensuous feelings introduced to her by Quintin Bell and the perverse, exciting sensations whispered in her ear by Alice Nell Puffin.   Then her thoughts were hit by the metallic sound of clicking and snapping.   Those sounds were quickly followed by the smell of smoke, muffled curses and water splashing as if someone was swimming.   She remembered kneeling on all fours rubbing her eyes along the grassy lip of the bunker to brush away more sand.   Her lips followed a return course along the grass.   She could hear a mixture of voices coming from over the raised lip of the sand bunker.   The voices were familiar and came from the direction of the croquet court. The voices faded in and out until only one voice remained.

Then there was the sound of a thunk. That was followed by two more thunks. She peered over the sand bunker's raised lip and saw what she wasn't sure she saw. Then she passed out face first in the grass.

Amanda Newton's MT had turned cold like her coffee. A telephone was glued to her left ear. Garbled mayhem sounding like two hung-over rugby teams playing in Grant Park on Sunday morning ripped through her ear. "Did you say your name was Mister Pepperwall and you want to talk with Tinker Bell?" she asked, trying to be polite. "I'm sorry, Sir, but I'm having an extremely difficult time understanding you. We must have a faulty connection." She listened, her eye brows seeming to climb up her forehead. "Mask?" she asked. "Sequins sprinkled where?" She looked at the mouthpiece of the phone and said: "Are you aware that this is a high school and it is Founder's Day?"

Bo's body quivered and shook as he squeezed the phone. "Lady, get the wax out of your ears!" he yelled into the mouthpiece of the antiquated black, dial phone that was on his pallet desk in his office. "Tell my Tinker Bell to get her big boobs down here pronto."

Amanda Newton removed the phone from her ear and stared disbelieving at it. Her eye brows climbed even higher. Demeanor and patience abandoned her. "Sir," she said, the phone placed back to her ear, indignance now her tone, "the only Tinker Bell we have in the Glen Forest on the Watercourse High School Library is in the book, Peter Pan." The phone jumped from her ear and almost out of her hand. "Oh, my, dearest Lord in Heaven," she said aghast. "Peter and Pan are doing what?" Her heart temporarily stopped. "Rubbing aloe lotion where?" Her heart started. "What harnesses?" The librarian never felt the phone slip from her hand or heard it drop uncharacteristically to its cradle with a plastic thud.

"Invest in a hearing aid, you deaf, old crow!" shouted Bo, his right hand squeezing the life out of the scarred, black relic, a dial tone the only reply to his order. "Cover charge," he shouted as if coming out of trance. "Quarters," he quickly added. "We need quarters for the movies in the Men's Room." He sprang up from the metal chair with the one rusted leg held together with duct tape and shouted, "Ice! Check to see if we have enough ice!"

Matilda Newton sat alone in the tiny dressing room that was also used by Peter, Pan and the six Go-Go dancers. She had no idea of a phone conversation that had gone on between Ben's uncle and her mother. If she had, she would've run out the fire exit door, jumped into the green water of the North Branch of the Chicago River and swam under water all the way to the locks in Wilmette. Her almost valedictorian status and National

Honor Society presidency hadn't prepared her for what was taking place during her senior year in high school. Wearing a leotard, black mask, thigh high boots and soaring from a ceiling in a special harness while tethered from a cable was not how she envisioned the highlight of her final year in high school. Being gawked at by a swarm of inebriated humanity wasn't something that appeared on the extra-curricular or co-curricular activities lists of application forms offered by prestigious colleges and universities. Her mother's alma mater, Vassar would surely shun her. Matilda, however, latched onto the new and glorious feeling that surged through her when she slipped on her black mask. Her dream was being fulfilled. She was in show business.

As frightened as Matilda was of her mother finding out about her string of white lies surrounding her ruse, she wouldn't change a second of her new and exhilarating life. Never before had she felt so important. Never in her life could she have imagined how the sound of shrill whistles and shouts of politically incorrect expressions coming from the lips of male customers excite her tender ears. Her secret fantasy, the one she embraced in the back room of the school library wearing head phones and listening to Ravel's, *Bolero*, was really happening. She was a perfect ten, walking along a pristine sand Mexican beach and accompanied by Ravel's background music. Well, almost. She wasn't in Mexico and the sensuous beat of the Bolero was missing, replaced by Cap'n's Kids' version of *Fly Me to the Moon*. None of that mattered to Matilda Newton now. She felt wanted. She felt important. She felt like she thought a Hollywood sex symbol felt and she loved it.

Ben made a coughing noise from the entrance to the dressing

room, his head sticking out from behind the Army surplus blanket door. "I'm proud of you," he said, not knowing what else to say. He had taken his late father's TR-3 that morning, the school closed for Founder's Day and picked up Matilda in front of Shake's Mortuary. Matilda, her excitement about performing again was curtailed by her fear of being discovered by her mother, listened to Ben.

"Honest," he said softly. "I overheard my mother tell Mr. Brown that Uncle Bo's discotheque was closing because it was bleeding to death, whatever that means." Ben wasn't aware of his uncle's noontime call to Matilda's mother or his frantic call urging Ben's mother to get downtown as fast as she could.

"Sis," Bo had screamed into the phone, "you ain't gonna believe this, but the gaggle I once told you about had multiplied faster than roaches in the slum across the street and they're crappin' a mountain of golden eggs that will bury Fort Knox!"

Ben was in no hurry to get Matilda to La Tinkerbelle's. She wanted to be there early so she could walk up to the bar, face her father and confess that she was Tinker Bell. She wasn't aware that he had given Bo his permission, although somewhat encumbered with threats, for her to be part of the discotheque's entertainment. Aware or unaware were the operative words exchanged by Bo and Sam; so were appropriate and inappropriate behavior. Bodily harm had been an expression used by Sam. The threat of bodily harm was followed by the possibility of Bo's death, according to Sam, "If one beautiful lock of my Princess' hair gets mussed up, I'll make sure you get the opportunity to meet Jesus." Sam had walked away from Bo thinking that his daughter would play the role of a pure and innocent character from a children's story.

"I have to tell my father, Ben," she said fidgeting with the seat belt in the TR-3's front seat. "Honesty is the best policy." Her eyes began to tear up. "Oh, Ben, I hope I don't lose my father again."

"You won't," said Ben comforting his girlfriend. "Sam's too cool of a dude to do that, "he said glancing at her. "Remember, it was your mother and that John Brown guy her divorce lawyer who made your dad look like an unworthy father." He looked back to the traffic in front of him. "Honesty, however, might have all of us joining my father in his grave," said Ben just as the TR-3 was forced to stop at the tail end of the biggest traffic jam he had ever seen. Horns honked and drivers stood, one foot in their car and the other on the pavement, trying to figure out what was holding up progress.

The answer was evident to Juan Ponce de Leone and his valet parkers. There were too many cars and way too many wild-eyed people leaving their cars, keys in them, to race across La Tinkerbelle's parking lot to wait impatiently pushing and shoving in another long line.

Ben, having learned the streets around La Tinkerbelle's from driving with his uncle so many times and also walking after taking public transportation, slammed the TR-3's gear shift in reverse, spun the steering wheel and executed a U-turn filled with grinding gears and peeling tires. The TR-3 bounded over a curb and sped for the bank of the Chicago River. Ben spun the wheel hard to the left as the hood of the car plowed through weeds that were taller than he and Matilda combined. The car's tires settled into a set of wide ruts cut along the river's bank by fisherman, joggers, lovers in search of privacy, drunks and a mugger or two. He spun the wheel again to the left, the car barely missing a Catalpa tree that had seen better days, a handful of anemic cigar like pods hanging down. The hood of the car emerged from another clump of tall weeds and sped into the jammed parking lot almost colliding with a car driven by Juan.

"Hey, amigo," shouted Ben. "What's going on?"

"Loco," said Juan, his index finger spinning in fast circles at his temple. He took the same index finger and pointed at the back of the discotheque. "Use the emergency door," he shouted, ramming down the accelerator of the Lexus he was parking and disappeared behind the building, the smell of abused tires hanging in the air.

Ben wasted no time. In moments the hood of the car was in the space marked with yellow diagonal lines and a *No Parking* sign mounted in front of them on the building's wall. He jumped out of the sport's car without opening the driver's side door and helped Matilda out. He watched as Matilda used her special entry technique on the emergency door. Her right knee applied pressure at a point exactly below where the inner latch was located; her slender fingers formed a familiar *V* and slid into a tiny opening above her right knee. The door popped open and a billowing cloud of stale booze, body odors and tobacco smoke crashed into them. That greeting was followed by the blare of amplified music they knew belonged to Rommie, Regis, Reggie and Obadiah. In a matter of seconds they both snuck behind the blanket that covered the dressing room used by the entertainers. They looked at each other in disbelief.

Ben finally said in a shout, "Maybe you should get into your costume."

Matilda blushed and said, "Ben, tell me I'm not one of those women," she said, her voice barely audible as it collided with the din coming from the main part of La Tinkerbelle's. "I'm not a," she said stopping and beginning to blush.

Ben looked puzzled.

"You know," Matilda continued, searching for the right words in a whisper. Her face was now glowing as she up the index and middle fingers of her right hand in a *V*.

Ben broke into a smile and nodded.

"Oh, Ben, you dufus," she said, frustration showing. "Don't make fun of me."

"What fun?" he repeated. "I don't see anything funny about wearing a black bathing suit that's sprinkled with silver glitter? The girls on our gymnastic team at school wear less."

"I don't know what my father's going to do when I tell him I'm your uncle's star attraction," she said, her eyes starting to well up. "I don't want to lose him again."

Ben put his hands on her shoulders and gave a gentle squeeze. "Don't worry about Sam," he said. "Just change into your costume and pray to the Almighty that your mother doesn't find out." He turned, looked back over his shoulder, gave her a smile and started for the blanket door. "I'll leave you ladies to your privacy."

Bo sat at his make-shift pallet desk still staring at the inert phone on his desk. He no longer wanted to choke the life out of it. He was at a loss. Amanda Newton had hung up on him.

CLICK/SNAP!

He blinked. The noise coming from the discotheque acted like an ammonia capsule had been snapped under his nose. "Cover charge," he muttered, a state of panic attacking him. He grabbed for his soiled white captain's jacket, buttoned the gold buttons ignoring the fact they were out of alignment and plopped his captain's hat on in a jaunty angle. "Forget the pants," he said, as he raced to the door. The maitre d' stand will cover me from the waist down. Got to get that cover charge," he kept repeating.

SNAP! CLICK!

Two steps out the door had him bumping into Peter and Pan. They had entered through the fire escape door, the door a scant false step from having a person exiting the club tumbling down a weedy embankment into the Chicago River. "Where's the sequins?" he asked, noticing that they were still dressed like the two kindergarten teachers.

"We just got here," said Peter, out of breath.

"The Rabbi's wife told us there was some kind of Pepperwall family emergency we had to get to," said Pan.

"There's your emergency," said Bo, nodding over his shoulder at the mob scene.

SNAP! CLICK!

"Your family is here," he said, looking wild eyed. "They're fine, you're fine and I'm fine. We're all family; a gang, you're my family and my gang," he said, his eye blink rate almost causing his lids to blister. "Now change and go help Juan park cars. But, glue on those sequins first and start soaring."

"Wow," said Peter, catching a glimpse of the crowded club.

"Where did all those people come from?" asked Pan, her scuffed leather shoulder bag with her school work slipping off her shoulder.

"From God," said Bo. "Heckle and Jeckle told a gossip columnist. How should I know? Maybe it was Hans; maybe one of his dogs. Schickle or Gruber, heck I don't know. Do something. Collect the money from the Men's Room stalls. Just don't stand there. The show must go on," he said blinking. "Sequins, ladies," he said, then began mumbling, "Go mash potatoes in the kitchen. Don't forget the cover charge."

"Mr. Pepperwall," said Peter, putting a hand on the sleeve of Bo's captain's jacket. "Whatever drugs you're on I want some. Wow!"

"Drugs?" asked Bo, his eyes now blinking so fast all he could see was a world of presidents' pictures, their images flashing by on old fashioned flip cards. "No. No drugs. Just get into those harnesses and bring Sam all the ice he can use. Oh, yeah, when you finish mashing the potatoes collect the quarters from the restroom. Hurry and get a move on. Yo-ho-ho and a bottle of Bacardi," he chanted. "There's no business like show business."

CLICK! SNAP!

Bo's head shot frantically from side to side. "Kids, we're going to put on a show. Tell Judy and Mickey."

"Are we still getting paid?" asked Pan.

"Double," yelled Bo. "Now get going. And don't forget the cover charge and a two drink minimum."

"We're going," said Peter, as she and her partner disappeared behind the wool blanket door of their dressing room stenciled with U.S. Army.

Bo inhaled, put down his head and resumed bulldozing his way through the mass of gawking bodies, pushing, shoving and goosing his way back toward the maitre d' stand shouting: "Cover charge! Cover Charge! Get your cover charge here!" He pushed, shoved and goosed some more and then heard a familiar voice.

"Watch where your pinching, you silly savage." It was Charles. He was with Frank trapped in the middle of the crowd. "Oh, Captain, my captain," said Charles, recognizing Bo and seeming to enjoy almost being crushed by the crowd. "Is this the good ship, Lollipop or what?"

"The boutique," Bo shouted back. "Get back in the damned boutique."

"We're trying, Boss," shouted Frank, his words coming out as if he had both lungs crushed. "We're trying to get back in after these maniacs pushed us out."

Charles grinned. "Where did all these people come from?" he asked.

"From God," yelled Bo, indicating that his two employees should follow him.

"Oh, goody," said Charles, an immense smile now covering everything on his face except his eye brows. "There is a God and that silly woman has answered my prayers." He put the back of his right hand to his forehead. "Oh, my, I'm feeling faint. I think I'm having an out of body experience." His right hand dropped down out of sight and a person next to him jumped. "So many posteriors, so little time."

"Read all about God and time in the paper," shouted Bo over his shoulder as he continued to push and shove. "It's on my desk. But get back into the boutique first. Double the prices of everything."

"Double...," Frank began to ask? He saw the wild look of determination on Bo's face. "Double it is, Captain Pepperwall."

Ben was standing outside of the dressing room when he heard Matilda call out his name. He peeled open the blanket making a slit, peered in and saw Matilda crying. "Matty, what's the matter?" he asked.

"I should have never told my mother I wanted to be on the stage."

"You told your mother about Uncle Bo and here?" he asked, feeling his knees begin to crumble.

"Not really," she said trying not to cry. "I mean, kind of." Her index fingers brushed at her tears. "I only mentioned something about acting and a possible part in Peter Pan." Tear drops filled her eyes again. "She never heard a word I said. She kept asking me all kinds of questions as if I were some kind of criminal. She wanted to know what kind of acting I would be doing. Then she mentioned Shakespeare, the classics and brought up legitimate theatre. She rambled on and on before telling me how majoring in theatre in college wouldn't be all that harmful as long as I had a double major in the Humanities with a minor in Latin."

"Latin," Ben mumbled. "How would you say, 'standing ovation' in Latin?" he asked. "Have you forgotten the applause after your debut?"

"Stantem ouans," replied the duet of Peter and Pan who had edged closer to Matilda to try and comfort her.

Ben gave Matilda a questioning look and asked, "Really?"

Matilda nodded, sniffled and said, "All of you will hear more than applause if my mother finds out what I'm doing."

She gave a sigh shrugged and said, "I guess it's time to get ready. The show must go on. Isn't that what they say in show business?"

Peter and Pan nodded.

"I didn't lie to my mother," added Matilda. "I did tell her I had a part between Peter and Pan." She paused. "We'll maybe I did tell a teeny tiny falsehood." She paused again. "I didn't insert the word, between when I mentioned Peter and Pan. Oh, and I forgot the word, and."

Arvia and John Brown couldn't believe the mob strung across the street blocking the entrance to the discotheque's parking lot. Caesar's Legions, four abreast and on the march, displayed more discipline than the lines stacked up at the front entrance to La Tinkerbelle's. Cars spilled out onto the sidewalks. In the back of the parking lot, two cars were nestled with their front bumpers submerged in the Chicago River, their emergency brakes holding the rest of the car on the bank. John Brown, hand jammed down on his BMW's horn, scattered Caesar's Legions and managed to get his BMW convertible on the sidewalk leading into La Tinkerbelle's parking lot. One of the valet parking attendants walked around to the driver's side window. His white shirt was minus half the buttons, one sleeve was almost torn off and his eye patch covered his left ear. "That'll be twenty dollars, Senor."

"Don't be ridiculous," said the attorney. "This is Mrs. Bell. She owns La Tinkerbelle's. She's your boss."

"Sorry, Senor, you're mistaken," said an apologetic Jesus. "Captain Bo and Donald Trump are de owners of dis place. Now twenty bucks please or go park over there." He used his thumb to indicate the housing project across the street where the attorney's car had once been stolen.

"Here you are, Jesus," said Arvia reaching across the attorney and handing a twenty dollar bill to the attendant. "It's so nice to see you again." She glanced at the parking lot. "I imagine that Juan and your other companions are busy as well."

"Oh, Senorita Arvia," said Jesus dropping his accent. "I'm sorry I didn't recognize you. Keep the double saw." He quickly sprinted around the front of the car and opened the door for Arvia. "Be careful," he said, nodding toward the building. "It's crazy in there." His index finger did a series of quick circles in the area of his right temple.

"I'll have your job, you arrogant Spic," the lawyer said, as he took Arvia by the arm and pulled her toward the club entrance. Then he heard the squealing of tires. Just as they both turned they caught a glimpse of the BMW before it rounded the corner of the building. There was an extended middle finger reaching up over the top of his car.

"I don't believe it," said Arvia, stopping abruptly to take another look at the mob of people shuffling in slow motion as they were funneled toward the main entrance of La Tinkerbelle's. "Where in heaven's name did all these people come from?"

"How should I know," said John Brown, unable to hide his agitation. "Knowing your brother he probably paid them to stand in line so his going, going, gone, gone business would look like it was thriving," he said, looking over his shoulder at the area where his car had once been stolen. "Donald Trump? Twenty bucks to park a car? Your brother is definitely nuts."

"Maybe he's not as nuts as you think, Mr. Brown," she said. "I think I see Noel working crowd control." She removed the attorney's hand from her arm and began to walk to the head of the line. That's when the shouts began.

"Hey, the line starts over in the projects," she heard, but ignored as she headed to where she saw Noel at the main entrance. She glanced to her left and saw Naomi waving at her from behind her showroom window. Arvia stopped, looked at Naomi and gave a shrug of her shoulders. Naomi did the same for her answer and was thankful for the temporary break offered by seeing a friendly face. She had been caught in the whirlwind of customers since coming into La Tinkerbelle's well before noon to tell Bo she was resigning. Then she found herself stacking paper hand towels in the restrooms; mixing drinks with Sam who allowed her behind the bar because of their experiences together at his defunct Working Man's Saloon and trying to get into her Captain Hookette costume. Her eye patch was pasted in the middle of her forehead by sweat and her phallic symbol artificial hook was sticking out of her bra. Arvia signaled ta-ta with her right hand and turned to hear John Brown say to someone waiting in line: "I'm with Arvia Bell. She's the owner of La Tinkerbelle's."

"Who gives a shit," was the reply from that someone who was waiting in line. "Wait your ass in line like the rest of us."

Just as Arvia and John Brown reached the entrance, four men in business suits burst out of La Tinkerbelle's front door.

They were laughing and staggering, but that didn't seem to matter to them as the four boisterous drunks collided with Arvia and the attorney almost knocking her down and spinning John Brown around like a top.

"Sorry about that, folks," said the first patron, his breath making Arvia's eyes water. "Are you hurt, Beautiful," he asked, his right hand making a brushing movement at Arvia's right arm, but missing it as he stumbled behind her and crashed into John Brown before landing on his knees. "They serve a helluva lunch in there, Gorgeous."

Beg your pardon, Sweetheart," said a second, wild eyed patron as he flopped his arm over the shoulders of a third companion who was deciding whether to sit down on the pavement or pass out. "You ain't lived until you had a slab of their meatloaf on pumpernickel with a slice of raw onion." He belched.

Arvia's nostrils puckered and John Brown saw the entrance to La Tinkerbelle's surrounded in a cloudy haze.

"Greatest lunch in the world, Pretty Lady," said the third patron deciding that sitting on the pavement was the prudent thing to do. He sat between his buddies, the first man now curled up like a combination Heckle and Jeckle once did at Arvia's feet when she had first encountered the cats when her brother first showed her the inside of the vacant factory several months earlier.

The fourth in the group staggered up to John Brown, put his hands on the attorney's shoulders, belched and asked proudly: "Sir, do you know what I had for lunch?" He didn't give John Brown time to answer. "I had pretzels, peanuts, and forty two shots of Rock 'n Rye. But who's counting?" Three of the men started giggling. The fourth snored. "Poor Shapiro can't count," continued the fourth, his hands sliding down John Brown's coat sleeves until his thumbs hooked into the lawyer's jacket pockets stopping his fall with a jerk. His neck tie flopped over his shoulder like an Ivy League scarf.

John Brown wanted to tell the men to get out of their way, but that would mean talking and talking would require breathing which would require inhaling. He chose to have his eyes keep watering while he waited for the men to get away from them.

"Shapiro can't count because he's sleeping," said the second man, nodding to the first lying on the pavement, his snoring intensifying. "I'm going to have a tough time explaining to his wife how he missed six trains."

"Six," repeated the first drunk, opening his eyes. "He only missed one. We had three hours to kill before we headed to Union Station." He burped. "Now we got 'til midnight." He burped again. "That's when the last choo-choo train chugs outta here."

"Blame your missed trains on your wanting to see those two celebrities get married in there," replied the second drunk. "Your wife will buy that. Hey, it's in the papers. Don't you believe everything you read?" They giggled out of control until one of the men asked his companions, "You guys wanna go back in for a nightcap?" They pulled their friend, Shapiro off the pavement and began yelling, "Taxi!"

John and Arvia watched as the men nodded what resembled an apology and moved on. Arvia reached down and picked up a newspaper one of the men had left on the ground. It was folded and open to the page where Izzy Inman's picture appeared at the top of his column. She couldn't miss the bold type spelling out La Tinkerbelle's. "Oh, my," she said, intending to keep heading for the door but finding her feet weren't moving as she concentrated on Izzy Inman's column.

John Brown kept looking over his shoulder to where Naomi Schmitt continued dancing and was instantly aroused. He walked back to the window, waved to get Naomi's attention, held up a hundred dollar bill and winked.

Two extended middle fingers was Captain Hookette's answer to John Brown's wink. She never missed a gyration.

Arvia spotted Noel just inside the door. The baby faced undercover cop looked haggard but stood erect and professional as he continued to snap up money out of midair. A red velvet rope hung across the main entrance, each end attached to a brass stanchion. She held up the newspaper and showed it to the cop. "Noel, what on earth," she managed to say.

"I don't have a clue, Miss Arvia," he said, releasing one end of the red velvet rope. "I got called off a drug stakeout to get here," he continued. He snatched a fluttering ten dollar bill out of the air then nodded in the direction of the maitre d' stand. "Two celebrities are supposed to get married in here today," he said looking puzzled. "I don't know who. Maybe your brother does."

Arvia followed Noel's glance down and saw Bo crawl out from under the maitre d' stand. His captain's uniform jacket that had once been sparkling and ready for inspection looked more beige and brown in color, darker stains merging into a jungle camouflage. Bo's eyes looked like two clear marbles and five, ten and twenty dollar bills sprouted out from all of the jacket's pockets like a rash of green weeds.

"Thank you, Noel" said Arvia, as she walked around the gold stand to join her brother. She ignored the shouts of, "Hey, bitch, who do you think you are?"

She stopped in back of the maitre d' stand, John Brown tucked in securely behind her. "Berthold," she said, ignoring more complaints from the customers waiting in line. "What in the world's going on here?"

"Welcome to La Tinkerbelle's, folks," said Bo, totally oblivious that he was talking to his sister. "That'll be ten dollars each for our cover charge. We're having a pre-nuptial special today."

"Berthold, are you okay," asked Arvia?

Bo blinked his eyes several times. "Bo okay," he said, sounding as if he were in a trance. "Bo more than okay," he continued. "Look around. Bo can't believe what Bo is seeing." He extended his empty right hand, his left crammed with money. "Bo wants ten dollars each for cover charge. Bo also makes change for men's room movies. How many quarters do you need?"

Arvia reached out and brushed her brother's arm. "Bo."

"Bo don't know why," he said, his eyes even glassier.

"Why am I not surprised," said John Brown, feeling the legal documents for closing La Tinkerbelle's, his passion for Arvia and his revenge slowly disintegrating in his suit coat pocket.

"Bo knows not why and Bo doesn't care. Read today's paper. That'll be ten dollars each." He paused, blinked several times and said, "Make that five dollars each. Today's double bonus point's day."

"Berthold Pepperwall," said Arvia questioning her brother's

charging her to enter her own business. Suddenly she found her face inches from the chest of a huge, muscular black man wearing what appeared to be a doorman's uniform and a black hat similar in style to Bo's. A gold chord fastened around his left shoulder stretched across his broad chest accentuating the uniform's glistening brass buttons. A sparkling silver whistle was clenched between his teeth. "Begging your pardon, madam," he said to Arvia as he flashed a smile of perfect white teeth. "My name is Charles. Charles Chuckwagon. I'm on my lunch break from the Drake Hotel and I need to speak to your commanding officer." He blew into the whistle twice getting weak peeps for his efforts. "Request permission to come aboard," he said to Bo, tossing him a salute that made him look like an officer in Her Majesty's Navy. His outstretched hand waved a ten dollar bill and he said, "If you'd be so kind, a roll of quarters, Commodore."

Bo appeared to snap out of his trance. "Permission granted," he said returning the salute then snatching the ten dollar bill from the customer's hand. "Quarters for you it is, Mr. Belafonte. It is Mr. Belafonte isn't it? I'm a captain. I outrank you."

"Aye-aye, Captain," said the uniformed man. You do indeed outrank me. You more than outrank that Belafonte gentleman you mentioned. I am not he," he continued respectfully as he reached out and took a roll of quarters. "I'm Head Door Man at the Drake. I have the rank of Concierge."

"If you're looking for a job in show biz," said Bo, glancing and nodding toward the bandstand, "I could use someone like you to sing. Do you know the Banana Boat Song?"

"No I don't, Captain. I'm more into Gospel Rap. Would you

like to hear my rendition of, Bite me, Bathsheba?"

"I prefer Banana Boats," said Bo. He glanced at John Brown and in an instant his eyes were flashing knife blades aimed at the lawyer. "Ten dollars for the lady and twenty for you for disrespecting our brave men in uniform like Concierge Chuckwagon here."

The waiting line snaking outside the main entrance surged forward pushing Arvia behind her brother and shoving John Brown up against the glistening gold painted maitre d' stand. The first man in the surge towered over John Brown and was crushing him into the wooden stand. His right arm stretched out over the attorney's head. "Beg your pardon, Admiral," he shouted to Bo. There was a hundred dollar bill in his hand. "I heard the four guys who just staggered out of here talking about porn films being shown in the Men's Room. Is that right?"

"Art movies," replied Bo taking the hundred dollar bill. "Would you like some quarters?"

"What kind of films?" asked Arvia over her brother's shoulder? "Did you say pornographic?"

"Yeah, Lady," said the man, his eyes lighting up, "you into porn?"

"How disgusting," Arvia managed to say.

"Don't knock it if you haven't tried it," said the man as he took two handfuls of quarters from Bo then nodded his thanks. "A little classy porn can liven up your sex life. And, from what I see, you could use some livening up."

The crowd gave another surge preventing Arvia from gouging the man's eyes out. Then she heard her brother.

"Ten for you lady and twenty for the barrister," said Bo

glaring at the lawyer. "Then, again, make that forty for you. That's another twenty for your car."

"What," spurted John Brown annoyed and angry? "Who in the hell do you think you are?"

"The owner," said Bo as he snapped to attention and gave the lawyer a salute.

Before the exchange became any more heated, Arvia opened her purse and pulled out a twenty dollar bill and a ten. "Is this adequate, Berthold?" she asked. She brushed the money under John Brown's nose before handing it to her brother. "I'm also the owner."

"Oh, take your money and shove...," said John Brown, stopping in mid sentence as Peter and Pan swooped down from the ceiling, the path of their arcs looking as if they were going to part his hair. He saw what looked like laser beams emanating from Arvia's eyes. "Shove it in some Salvation Army kettle."

Arvia turned and caught a glimpse of Sam behind the bar. "I'm going to say hello to Sam," she said to her brother.

Bo smiled then glared at John Brown. "No cameras allowed in the Men's Room," he snapped.

John Brown wanted to kill.

Arvia began to force her way through the crowd toward the bar, the frustrated, confused and growing angrier lawyer following her.

"You owe me forty bucks!" shouted Bo to the attorney who ignored him.

Sam flipped a quick wave in Arvia's direction signaling for her to come to the end of the bar. His hands returned to a blur of activity as ice cubes rattled into glasses from one hand and a continuous stream of liquor rained from rapidly changing bottles in his other. He never spilled a drop.

Arvia watched as one of the waiters, at Sam's direction, placed a bar stool up to the bar. She didn't see the customer who had been sitting on the stool now laying flat on his back, his on-the-rocks glass resting on his stomach.

"Sam!" shouted Arvia, the look on her face asked her question.

Sam gave a shrug; his hands still a blur, liquor pouring out of two different bottles into two different glasses. "That Izzy Inman columnist guy wrote a story in today's Examiner about two celebrities who were getting married in here today."

"Married in here today?" repeated Arvia. "In La Tinkerbelle's a Go-Go?"

A nod came from Sam as he packed four glasses with ice cubes. In a flash, two more bottles appeared from their location in the stainless steel well beneath the bar, labels of unheard of brands partially covered by his hands. "Inman's column was something about a TV prostitute and a smut peddler, Mrs. Arvia." He stopped, grabbed two more bottles and continued pouring drinks. "I'm not sure what the article was about. I thought I read something about a preacher. I thought I saw pornography mentioned. Heck, I'm not sure. All I know is that your brother went from deep depression into a state of hyperactivity. He looks like he's in this wild-eyed trance.."

"Pornography," asked Arvia in a whisper? "That's the second time today I've heard my name being linked to filth and the dregs of the earth?"

John overheard Arvia's questions and said to Sam: "Did I hear you mention a prostitute, smut peddler and pornography?"

"Watch your language around the lady," said Sam, his right

hand reaching under the bar, his fingers tracing the solid handle of his custom made electric cable black jack.

"What's it to you," said John Brown. "I'm talking to the lady. You know, the owner, your boss, the one who does the hiring and firing. The lady wants to know what's going on here."

"Read the papers, Mr. Lawyer Man," said Sam. He glared at John Brown. "Oh, I forgot, all you know how to do is serve papers." Sam looked at Arvia, the glare gone replaced by a look of respect. "What would your Honor like to drink?" he asked, using the title of respect to Arvia who had followed her late husband into the Glen Forest on the Watercourse mayor's office.

"She'll have...," John Brown started to say.

"Excuse me, Sir," said Sam, the cold abruptness in his voice giving the attorney an eerie feeling he didn't like. "I'm waiting on her Honor the Mayor."

"Thank you, Sam," Arvia said. Her voice almost a shout. "You know what I like Sam," she said with a polite smile, "One of your champagne cocktails."

"But, Arvia you know what champagne...," said John Brown before getting cut off again, this time by Arvia.

"I'd like a champagne cocktail," she said to the lawyer, her nose almost brushing up against his. "Champagne doesn't affect me. Maybe you were thinking about how it affects the pastor's wife or maybe the Chief of Police's wife or perhaps your parade of secretaries named after Disney characters."

"One champagne cocktail for the Boss," said Sam, his face down, eyes concentrating on his work, his hands in line with his homemade black jack under the bar.

"And I'll have a Bombay gin martini straight up with an

onion," said John Brown. "That drink, for your edification, is called a Gibson. And, since I'm with the owner, I believe the customary thing to do is to comp our drinks."

"You are almost correct, Sir," said Sam. "The lady is the owner and her cocktail is on me. You, however, owe me twelve dollars for the Gibson. That's in advance."

Amanda Newton, her tolerance level needle buried in the red danger zone from standing in bumper-to-bumper traffic two blocks from La Tinkerbelle's, whipped the steering wheel of her seven year old red Monte Carlo, her foot jamming down on the accelerator pedal. The sporty Chevy appeared show room new having been taken from its parking spot behind Shake's Mortuary and driven only on Sundays, and that to church. Amanda opted to walk to her job at the high school as part of her daily fitness regimen, an Alpine style back pack slung over her shoulder containing equipment for all emergencies ranging from tornadoes to avalanches to an extra package of Raman noodles for lunch. The car lurched into action picking up screaming speed as the librarian pointed the Monte Carlo into the oncoming traffic lane. It was impossible for her to hear the collective, startled cries of, "Oooooh," punctuated with colloquialisms covered with fear echoing from the motorists who were staring at the Chevy's hood closing in on them. Their assorted fearful cries beginning with, "Oh, shit" or "What the…" were joined by a crescendo of screeching brakes, honking horns and looks of fright and panic by stricken motorists and pedestrians trying to avoid colliding with the oncoming red missle.   In a matter of seconds, cymbals and percussion instruments exploding, Amanda Newton whipped the steering wheel again and the car bounded into the parking lot of La Tinkerbelle's.

"No one calls me a cow and gets away with it," she yelled at one of Juan's dazed attendants. Her foot jammed down on the accelerator again as she propelled the car's left hand side over a protective speed bump at the edge of the driveway entrance. Impatient drivers waiting for the valet parking service forgot about impatience and instantly thought of survival.

The red Monte Carlo went into a half spin, bounced once to the left and back again to the right barely missing the red and white security gate arm. Amanda jammed her foot down on the brake almost pushing the pedal through the floor board. The red missle came to a screeching, ear splitting stop that almost pinned Juan and Jesus against the driver's side of the car. She pushed the down button of her window and looked into the two petrified eyes of Juan and Jesus, the other two eyes covered by pirate patches.

"Twenty dollars, pleeze," said a rattled Juan, sweat drenching his bandana and steam rising from his soaked shirt. Jesus looked like a new cadaver in Loyola's Medical School lab. He held up his right hand with two fingers forming a *V*.

"Outrageous," said Amanda Newton, her finger poking so hard at the up button of her window that she broke both a finger nail and heard the first joint of her finger pop. Her other hand simultaneously shifted the car into Drive. At the same time, Juan's fingers rode the window up and into the weather seam channel of the door frame. The look of fear on his face made no difference to her. She saw an empty parking space in front of her and her foot jammed down on the accelerator. The space she was headed for was barely big enough for Naomi Schmitt's Peugeot which sat to one side of the area.

"Madre!" screamed Juan as he was pulled along, his fingers locked into the seam between the glass and the window channel, his look of fear changing to one of his impending demise.

"Twenty dollars indeed," said Amanda Newton to no one in particular. She spun the steering wheel and Juan started praying in Spanish to Our Lady of Guadalupe. "Of all the nerve," she said to the frightened face pleading with her on the other side of the window. "For twenty dollars I'll park my own car." She saw one eye screaming out fear and an open mouth that wanted to say the same thing, but couldn't. Her foot smashed down on the brake as the car made a perfect entrance between the Peugeot's dented passenger side, her passenger side missing La Tinkerbelle's brick wall by an inch.

Juan thanked Our Lady of Guadalupe as Amanda Newton lowered the window on her side, his fingers still wedged in the weather channeling. She opened the door, got out and looked down at Juan who was on his knees, his uncovered eye looking to the heavens. "Where's Berthold Pepperwall?" she demanded.

Juan nodded toward the entrance. "Captain Bo he is in dare."

Amanda, her Alpine pack slung over her shoulder, stepped over Juan's feet and started jogging to the main entrance where the lines were still four abreast and stretching across the street.

She didn't hear the prayers of thanksgiving from Jesus who was pinned between the car and a howled out space in the brick wall that was designed to hold a large garbage dumpster.

Amanda ignored the lines, her knees pumping as if she were running through two feet of snow. There were cries of, "Hey lady! Where do you think you're going?" and, "Who in the hell do you think you are?"

Amanda, on a mission, ignored them. She couldn't ignore, "End of the line, bitch!" Her knees continued to pump, one pump ramming into that particular patron's crotch. He hit the pavement with a thud, doubled up on the black top pavement. "That's no way to address a Vassar graduate and a librarian!"

Amanda Newton was stopped by Noel and his velvet rope. "I'm sorry, Mam," said Noel politely, "but there will a short wait for seating. The City of Chicago has a limit as to how many patrons are allowed into a confined space."

"I'm looking for Berthold Pepperwall," said Amanda Newton in a tone that had Noel shifting into his riot control mode. "And where's my daughter, Matilda?" she asked.

Her tone had Noel going down his check list of options for dealing with an irate female. "I'll look into that for you, Mam," said Noel politely. "Wait here and I'll be right back."

Ben, after leaving Matilda in the dressing room with Peter and Pan, found himself crouching down at the end of the bar trying to hide from his mother and John Brown. His eyes and the top of his head were the only things visible. He couldn't help but admire the way Sam worked, his speed and efficiency mesmerizing him. His fascination didn't last long when he saw Matilda's mother standing at the maitre d' stand. She did not look pleased. Then he saw Noel approach her, say something, or tried to say something. That conversation lasted less time than it took Ben to duck down and try to hide. Noel turned and started into the crowd. Had Ben not scampered for cover he would've seen Matilda's mother turn bright red, hook her thumbs under the straps of her back pack and shove her way through the crowd after Noel. Before Ben could crawl under the bar and hide, Matilda's mother was next to him. She was not happy. Neither was Noel. He was scared.

"Benoni," said an irate Amanda Newton looking down at him, "your mother allows you in a place like this?"

"It's a fine place, Miss Newton," said Ben. He looked up and tried to smile. "It's where the classics are performed. I even hear some of the employees talking in Latin."

"Indeed!" blurted out Matilda's mother. "That rude, filthy, dirty man in the parking lot pan handling me for money didn't speak in Latin."

"That's Juan, Miss Newton," said Ben politely. "He speaks Spanish and Latin." He tried to stand up and hit his head on the solid arm rest of the bar. "He's the parking lot manager."

"Manager indeed," she said disgusted. "And who in the names of Melpomene and Thalia is that poor excuse for a thespian in the window at the front entrance?"

"That's Naomi, Mrs. Newton," said Ben, his politeness staying in high gear. "She's a social worker. Helps crack babies." He thought he had a plan, but now he didn't know what he was going to do or what he was going to say once Matilda's mother saw her daughter soaring across the ceiling of La Tinkerbelle's. "Naomi's a respected professional," he continued as he tried to take a more scenic route before facing the inevitable firing squad. "She also helps the elderly, the poor and the street people. Her dancing brings her extra money for the needy." He paused to catch his breath. "I heard her speak Latin."

"Latin," huffed Amanda Newton. "Dressed like that?"

"I'll explain later," said Ben. He rubbed his head and looked at Noel who was now standing a safe distance from Matilda's mother. "Hey, Noel, what's happening?" he asked, trying to buy time as he calculated his escape route. "This is Matilda's mother," said Ben, his eyes flashing a warning that didn't go unnoticed.

Noel nodded and smiled. "Mam," he said over the noise in the disco, "I just noticed Mr. Pepperwall's return to the maitre d' stand." He nodded in the direction of the wave of humanity surging back and forth at the front entrance.

"I'll take Matilda's mother to him," said Ben, thinking that the front entrance would make an excellent escape route. "Too many people there for me to get shot at," he thought as he offered his arm to Amanda Newton and said: "Hang on."

Bo, still wild eyed, saw his nephew escorting a woman wearing a backpack toward him. "That'll be ten dollars each cover charge."

"Uncle Bo, it's me."

"Ten dollars each, please," said Bo again without a blink. He looked at Amanda Newton and quickly added, "Would you like a job? You'd look spectacular in a black sequined leotard and that backpack." His eyes did a quick up and down trip of the front of Amanda Newton. "Mmmm," he murmured. "How would you and your backpack like to be movies?" He lifted his eye patch and nodded his approval. "You'd cause a sensation in the men's room." His eye patch flapped back down and he seemed to return to his trance.

Amanda's face flushed and, for whatever reason, she didn't reach into her backpack for her can of mace.

Ben waved his hand in front of his uncle's face. "Uncle Bo, it's me, Ben. Are you okay?"

Bo blinked several times then shook his head. "Benny Boy, what are you doing here? Why aren't you in school where you belong?"

"Because there's no school today, Uncle Bo," he said. "I have a free day."

"Nothing's free, Benny Boy," said Bo, stuffing money under the maitre d' stand, kicking at a few, loose errant bills that spilled down from the mountain of money in the cardboard liquor box. "Is this charming lady a friend of yours?"

"This is Miss Amanda Newton," said Ben slowly. "She's our school's librarian. She's my friend, Matilda's mother," you know" he continued, trying to make eye contact with his uncle to warn him. "She suggested I read Peter Pan." He turned and faced Matilda s mother. "Didn't you, Miss Newton?"

"Yes, I did," she muttered. "Peter Pan, I believe so." She appeared pensive for a moment and said, "There certainly appears to be an excessive amount of interest in Peter Pan nowadays."

"My nephew is so very fortunate to have such a lovely, dedicated educator serving his every academic need." said Bo.

CLICK/SNAP!

"That'll be five dollars each cover charge," said Bo with a cordial smile. "That's my special discount for members of the teaching profession. Can't do enough for our teachers I always say."

Ben cringed. "You can't charge Matilda's mother to get in."

"I charge, me charge, we charge," he said. "Vini, vidi, vici," he continued appearing proud of himself. "That's Latin you know."

"This is Peter Pan's mother," said Ben, blurting out the name.

"Who?" asked Amanda Newton.

"So pleased to meet you, Mrs. Pan," said Bo, taking Amanda's hand and giving it a kiss. "Any friend of my nephew is a friend of mine. And, you are most certainly welcome here at the world's most exclusive and famous night club." He blinked. "Nephew, take this lovely lady to the bar and introduce her to Sam." He paused and snatched a twenty dollar bill from a grandfatherly looking patron who had a female companion thirty years his junior glued to his side. "Hope you and your niece enjoy La Tinkerbelle's," he said, then turned his attention back to Amanda Newton. "Ben, escort Mrs. Peter to the bar."

"Uncle Bo," said Ben cautiously. "You're talking to Mrs. Newton, as in Matilda. You know, the..." He held up his right hand again to simulate ringing a bell, "tinkle, tinkle, Tinker Bell."

"Oh, you're that Mrs. Hook, "said Bo. "Don't you have your daughter, Hookette working for me in our showcase window in front?"

CLICK/SNAP!

"How silly of me," Bo babbled on. "Forget the five dollar cover charge."

CLICK/SNAP!

"But, Uncle Bo," mumbled Ben."

"No buts, nephew."

"Only my butt," muttered Ben, Matilda's mother and his uncle not hearing him. He turned to Matilda's mother. "If you'd like, Mrs. Newton, I'm sure Sam can find you a seat at the end of the bar so you can be comfortable while waiting for the show to begin." He swallowed and let out a sigh. "Curtain goes up again, I think, in a few moments. He tried to force a smile, but the smile wouldn't be forced. "Curtains for me," he said, his voice hushed. Several shoves and a few pushes on Ben's part paved the way for Matilda's mother. They reached the far end of the curved bar where Sam, head down, was still a flurry of activity.

Sam looked up for a second and wiped his hands on a spotless white apron. "Ah, Master Ivy Leaguer, did you ever think you'd see the day with so many people would be packed into your uncle's dream?"

"Did I hear that a newspaper column caused all of this?" asked Ben, reaching across the bar and shaking hands with Sam. Ben swallowed what he felt would be his last living swallow and said to Sam: "Sam, I'd like you meet Mrs. Newton, Matilda's mother. You know." He started to do his bell ringing pantomime again, but didn't get past the first tinker.

"Hi, Mandy, long time no see."

Lucia Gunderson flipped the copy of the Examiner on the ornate desk top in her new school office. Izzy Inman grinned up at her. The names, Pepperwall and Bell jumped out at her as did the name, John Brown, Attorney at Law. As Lucia Gunderson read it aloud she said, "That lousy camera holding pervert." Her mind raced as she rescanned Izzy Inman's column. Arvia Bell's named jumped out at her. "That bitch as Mayor ain't gonna do me one bit of good," she muttered at the article, her New England lisp more pronounced than ever. She looked at her lone Angel fish who she had nicknamed QB, knowing she was the only one who knew the initials belonged to the late Mayor Bell. But her memories of Quintin Bell had become vague recollections of amorous interludes shrouded with steam and fish tanks. Memories, she knew, weren't going to help her reach her ultimate goal, and Mayor Arvia Bell certainly wasn't. "Survival of the fittest," she said to her garishly decorated office that Mayor Quitin Bell referred to as the Principal's Pushy-pushy-Play Pen. An evil tainted smile angled across her mouth, her lame eye trying to hop on board. "I'm at that bitch's mercy, but not for long." Her good eye danced, the lame one following several steps behind. "And you're going to help me climb the ladder of success, aren't you, John Scats Brown, my horny crime photographer." She picked up the Examiner and it quivered in her hands. She winked at a smiling Izzy Inman and tossed the paper into her ornate wrought iron waste paper basket with the sculpture of a Peregrine falcon, a tiny rodent clutched in its talons. "Scats, with very little effort I can get you to be Mayor of this fair community once I get that Arvia bitch bounced from office." She let out a laugh. "And that won't be hard now that she's up to her double chin in scandal. Your first duty, Scats will be to appoint me President of the School Board." She smiled and said, "Bye-bye, Rodney you poor shaggy bird dog," referring to the current School Board President. "How does it feel to be out of a job?"

Principal Gunderson reached for her phone and dialed Transportation. She was going to see La Tinkerbelle's first hand, in style, using the school district's limousine. The phone rang for an eternity before she realized that the only person in the building besides herself was one of the maintenance men. She never bothered to check the library. "It's a damned holiday," she muttered as she traipsed down to the boiler room area of her school where she found Hermie Goering, the custodian eating his lunch, a braunschweiger sandwich on caraway dark rye washed down with a diet Dr. Pepper. Hermie informed her that he did not have the keys to the school vehicles and the only form of transportation she could get was the little yellow school bus that was washed, filled with gas and waiting for the morning run the next day. In order for her to get the keys she needed the police department's permission. Lucia smiled here crooked smile, thanked Hermie and returned to her office. "Police, indeed," she said, dialing a number she had memorized. Two rings had Linda Ann Finn, the police chief's wife, jumping at Lucia Gunderson's invitation to drive into Chicago to see La Tinkerbelle's. Glen Forest on the Watercourse was not a hub of the performing arts, social outlets and cabarets. Outside of the annual ice cream social in front of the mortuary in the town square, the police department's Fourth of July Pancake breakfast and the Fall Pumpkin Fest with the crowning of Miss Gourd of the Glen, the village zipped up its streets when the sun went down.

If two were company, Lucia Gunderson found that Linda

Ann Finn suggested inviting Wanda Mensch and Margret Farnsworth Pepperwall Jones along for the ride. It was an invitation, she felt, would help solidify her plans for upward mobility and all but guarantee her becoming President of the School Board. Both ladies, according to Linda Ann, were long time residents dedicated to the community and a trip to see the latest rage attached to their town would be a nice gesture and, as Lucia Gunderson quickly surmised, a way to get on the good and right sides of the town's real power brokers. Before Lucia realized, the little yellow bus had two more passengers; Pastor Rufus Puffin and his wife Alice Nell.

Lucia Gunderson paid no attention to the traffic around La Tinkerbelle's. She double parked the little yellow school bus in front of the housing project high rise, put on her emergency flashers and let her passengers out the rear emergency door.

The lines to get in La Tinkerbelle's were still stretched across the street but that didn't matter to the five women and one man dressed in his best Harris Tweed sport coat and clerical collar. Pastor Puffin, his worn, tattered Bible in hand, led his cadre of soul savers past the long lines singing, "Onward Christian Soldiers." Alice Nell literally brought up the rear, her swaying figure attracting souls. How many of those souls were for saving wasn't on her mind. Into La Tinkerbelle's they marched, their path blocked by a velvet rope and a startled Noel Jones who called out, "Grandma!"

CHAPTER 4

<u>Bust, Bonanza, Boutique and Blaze</u>

If the crowd that was about to bust out the walls of the foundry converted to a discotheque was amazed at what they were experiencing, that couldn't compare with what Bo, Sam, Ben, his mother, Matilda, her mother and Noel Jones were experiencing. The last person Noel Jones expected to ask for a cover charge was his grandmother. He didn't get the chance.

Even the din inside La Tinkerbelle's couldn't cover the shrill cry that echoed from the boutique. Charles had struck again and Frank wasn't pleased.

Frank's relationship with Charles had been like a second rate soap opera since the day they met in Schmendel's Delicatessen, a happenstance meeting almost erupting into a catastrophic fist fight and a near death experience for Charles. Actually, it was Frank punching Charles in the shoulder after Charles had shoved him away from Schmendel's old fashioned pickle barrel where the last surviving kosher dill floated waiting to be snatched up for someone's lunch. Charles's shove amounted to Frank being moved two to three inches off vertical in front of the barrel. The shove had been one of Charles's all-time great assertive efforts at establishing his prowess with the Marques of Queensbury's rules of pugilism; all other attemptss having failed with humiliating results. This time humiliation came in the form of a punch to his shoulder and a brief verbal thrashing of three words: "Manners, Tinker Bell." Little did either realize how that reprimand would change their lives.

Frank got his pickle; he loved garlic dill pickles, and what the Schmendel brothers created in brine was his heaven. Charles, on the other hand, after threatening to call the police on who he referred to as: "You ill dressed discard on the editorial floor of GQ," went into a fit. A fit for him consisted of hands clenched in fists; his cheeks puffed out and his eyes closed as he held his breath for what seemed to him knocking on death's door for all of six seconds. Then he released his breath with what sounded like a weak *phew* and said: "Take that, Franco." After Frank stopped laughing, Charles, hands on hips, stated: "Your barrister will be hearing from my barrister." There was a pause followed by another *phew* and a second threat: "I hope you have millions in insurance because you're going to need it." His hands and arms quickly folded across his chest and he ended their initial meeting with, "So there!" Then he snatched the pickle from Frank's hand and ran out the delicatessen door.

Both Schmendel brothers looked at each other and then at Franco. "Don't worry one of the Schmendel's said. "We were just going to roll out a fresh barrel." The other Schmendel said, "So, that's what a real live Putz looks like."

Charles had returned to the delicatessen minutes after that first near death experience, apologized to the owners, paid for the pickle which he had eaten and then said to Frank, "The least you could do is walk me to my flat after that vicious pummeling you gave my arm you sweet, Franco, you." He put his left hand to his forehead and said, "You insensitive brute have caused me to feel oh so light of head and my right hand shakes as if I have the palsy." He held out his right hand and made it quiver. "It's so embarrassing," he said to Frank. "People see my hand moving and they must think that I'm engaging in some form of sexual self abuse."

Other near death experiences followed for Charles on a daily basis in the love-hate relationship he had fabricated. Those couldn't compare with what Frank was now sensing. Pummeled was a misnomer for what the afternoon throng that had invaded La Tinkerbelle's was doing to him at the entrance to the boutique. Death was more than near. Life, as he knew it, was about to come to an end. He had heard about golden images and glowing lights; signs welcoming newcomers into the hereafter. Hideous characters flashed by him in the dazzling lit tunnel where he felt trapped like an accused warlock at a Salem witch trial. Characters with ugly faces and uglier laughs were going by him so fast he'd never be able to know whether his hero, Dudley Do-Right would get there in time to rescue him. "C'est la vie," he muttered, as he squeezed his chunky body behind the boutique's chrome metal accordion security gate knowing that a single crowd surge would leave his remains looking like a *Ihop* waffle for all eternity. That, he felt, was better than being stampeded to death by a herd of crazed souvenir hunters. He couldn't believe he was in the eye of mass hysteria. "Maybe if I'm lucky," he thought, "I'll just be minus a limb or two. I wouldn't mind spending the rest of my remaining years in a full body cast urinating through a tube into a plastic bag." He shut his eyes and waited for the inevitable.

Charles wasn't waiting to die. He was protecting himself from who he felt were crass human beings minus all evidence of social redeeming values. On his hands and knees, he cowered behind the boutique's glass display counter, trembling, his head hidden under the cash register till, the drawer sitting open. His arms hugged his knees in a death grip. Rage joined his tears. He watched everything that he had so meticulously hung on hangars and put on display earlier being clutched in claws, paws or jaws. He watched in choked horror as the designer clothing underwent a massive test of the materials' tensile strength being applied by the brute force of savages. The only evidence of his show room merchandising display perfection was several empty matching pink plastic hangars clattering on the chrome display racks like homeless waifs. He could no longer blame Franco for what he saw was a rape of his rigid, anal retentive standards. "Dear, God," he mumbled, "protect me from those vicious swine in this the hour of my need."

Frank gave up the security of the chrome accordion door after being bounced against the wall several times, the accordion door putting his predicted impressions on his body so that barbeque grill marks joined his impersonation of a giant waffle. He slithered out of the side opening and, before he knew it, found himself on the floor being trampled by a mob worse than a swarm of paparazzi. No self-respecting apostle of William Randolph Hurst with a collection of lenses dangling around their neck would miss a prospective feeding frenzy.

Catching images of human beings about to be sliced and diced into fish chum was what careers in the media were made of.

Frank crawled on his hands and knees until he was next to Charles who looked at him through teary eyes, his hands and arms flailing away at his partner while he ordered: "Out, out you Brutus Maximus. Find your own damned spot." Then he tried to push Frank out of the way. Frank didn't budge under the feeble push and Charles fell backwards, his head and shoulders hitting the wall. "You're no better than those etiquette challenged barbarians," he said, rubbing at a pretend bump on his head.

"Queer today, gone tomorrow," muttered Frank, as he tried to stand up, the cash register's open drawer meeting his head. He looked at Charles in pain. "Why didn't you close the damn drawer?"

Charles smiled, his face flashing, "That's why."

Frank slammed the cash register's drawer shut with such force that he almost sent the entire computerized mechanism sailing off the end of the counter. When he looked up he was greeted by shouts of, "I'm next!" All he could see were hands filled with money, the money being shoved in his face. He wasted no time and snatched bills out of the sea of waving hands. Price tags were meaningless to him. He knew the prices of everything in the boutique. When money swatted his face he doubled the price and pretended to make change. Several coins spilled through his fingers into an outstretched hand, some change hitting the glass counter top. No currency was given back as Frank stated over and over: "Thank you. All sales are final. Thank you. Next." He stuffed money into his front and back pants pockets. Currency found its way into his underwear and socks. "Thank you," he kept shouting, until he was hoarse, repeating that all sales were final, adding, "No refunds. No exchanges."

The customers didn't care. This was an historic moment; bigger than shoppers caught in a death stampede or being shot on Black Friday as they fought like gladiators in the Roman Coliseum for a flat screen television made with Asian slave labor. Christ being kept in Christmas didn't matter. There was money to be made. Not as much money as a Mexican drug trafficking operation, but plenty thanks to two celebrities, two of the most often mentioned and photographed people to grace the front page of the tabloids. Rumors of a marriage between two stars, the duo deciding to get married in La Tinkerbelle's and having an opportunity to witness the nuptials, was what made life in America worth living. This was the horse player's equivalent of winning the Daily Double; bigger than cashing in a lottery ticket consisting of high seven figures. This was bigger than the Miracle of Fatima; the U.S. Olympic hockey team beating Russia, bigger than even the introduction of the first Edsel and even bigger than seeing Elvis from the hips down for the first time courtesy of the Ed Sullivan Show. A celebrity wedding taking place in the newest, hottest, trendiest club in the world and covered by the media was what dreams were made of. Souvenirs, real souvenirs with real meaning, didn't pop up for sale every day, especially not across a country drowning in, "Made in China" junk cramming the shelves of Marts—K, Wall, Quick and Mini. Izzy Inman's readers knew they were about to witness something bigger than the second coming of Christ. He had told his readers that there would be a grand and glorious wedding, a marriage for the ages and Izzy never mislead his readers. At times he may have exaggerated, but he never allowed a falsehood to leave his computer.

Money continued to be waved in Frank's face, each bill shouting, "Take me! Take me! I'm next!" Frank kept taking and kept repeating his line about no exchanges and no refunds.

Still on the floor behind the counter, his head resting against the wall was Charles in full snit. A resigned sigh complete with a silent movie star's theatrics drifted from him after seeing his display racks begging for mercy. "Don't step on me," he heard the chrome racks cry. He got to his knees, looked up at Frank, tugged on his pant leg and said: "Obviously I could wait until doom's day before some ruder than rude soul is going to apologize for inflicting severe bumps and bruises about my person."

Frank, both of his hands jammed with money, unleashed the bills and, without looking down at Charles, ordered: "Stuff these into your Fruit-of-the Looms, Pola Negri and be quiet."

Charles let out a huff and began sorting the bills. "Heads to the top," he said out loud. "One, two, five, ten, twenty, fifty and one hundred," he continued, just loud enough to annoy Frank. "No, no, no never, never allow a folded corner," he said, sounding frustrated, his fingers smoothing each of the bills. Just as he was about to count and check that his money stack was sorted correctly, another shower of bills rained down on him. "Damn, damn, double damn you, Wolf Man," he said, using a nickname reserved for rare periods of stress. The first stack of bills Charles counted did indeed find their way past the waist band of his burnt orange, silk thong. They were quickly arranged in a bulge behind his fly. "May every night cast a full moon on your rude, crude hairy soul," he said to his partner.

His sorting process continued as he tried to ignore the crazed throng who continually battered the glass counter causing it to tip toward them before bouncing back. "Oh, my goodness gracious," he said flustered, using his mother's favorite expression. "Keep that up and there'll be no treat for you before bedtime."

Frank glanced down for a moment before unloading another shower of bills on Charles. Several bills drifted out to the edge of the counter.

Charles grabbed the bulk of the money in one hand and leaned out on his hand and knees to pull in the stray currency. His vision went out of focus and he clutched at his right hand with his left, the money pressed against the top of his hand. Severe pain spread across his face. "Hey, Nancy Sinatra," he shouted, as his over bite dug into his skinny lower lip. "Watch where your boots are walking, Bitch!"

Frank kept plucking money from hands and simulating the whirling ring of the cash register by pressing his tongue against the roof of his mouth and making a blowing sound. After a dozen imitation rings, he literally threw the money on the floor. He glanced down when he didn't hear a complaint from Charles. He saw Charles holding his hand, his face in agony, tears filling his eyes. "We already have a real Tinker Bell performing here, Miss Rigby," he said, his attention returning to taking money. "That hand is three feet from your heart," he yelled, his yell followed by several false cash register rings. "Take out your pain on those poor presidents lying on the floor behind me." Suddenly, Frank found himself being shoved off to the side. "What the," he muttered as he saw Charles standing in his place.

Charles was smiling and taking money, a polite thank you accompanying each bill that found his hands. In an effortless move, he handed the bills to a dumbfounded Frank.

Frank knew that only one thing could make Charles go from pain to pleasure faster than a heartbeat. That one thing was a pair of cruising eyes on the make. In this case, it was a dozen pairs of eyes, not all on the make, but enough to bring out his partner's flirtatious best.

"Bonanza, Franco, my ex-best friend," said Charles. He had recognized a group of athletic looking men with dark complexions who he had heard were members of a visiting professional soccer team from Mexico. They were in Chicago to play a local team in a charity game. "Oh, my, what should a poor boy do?" he said. Not a soul heard him as the money continued to pile up on the floor behind the counter like drifts from a green, paper blizzard. He started to tell customers the cost of their purchase in Spanish trying to impress whoever the soccer players might be. He only knew how to say, "Uno" and "tres," in Spanish along with several other phrases that might produce a telephone number. Ramon in his hair styling salon next to the boutique had amassed a collection of six phone numbers and made sure Charles knew.

Frank, now sitting on the floor, collected, sorted and folded money at a frenzied pace. He was a man of his word, at least when it came to running the boutique. No unruly mob would get the best of him. He looked up for a moment, got hit in the face with a hundred dollar bill and stuffed it and the others in his shirt pocket.

"Gracias," said Charles, his smile almost swallowing his ears as he took another bill. Without looking he dropped it on

Frank. "Me allmo, Carlos," he said, shifting all of his gears into cruising mode. "Shot and a score anyone?" he asked.

"Do your job, Pele," ordered Frank, his words showing that he was becoming more than annoyed with Charles. "Don't touch the customers," he ordered.

"Oh, touch this," replied Charles, his middle finger extended down and hidden from the wall of customers in front of him by the counter.

Frank reached up, grabbed the middle finger and gave it an angry twist.

Every head in the discotheque focused on the boutique and the excruciating noise that drew the attention of the tenants in the public housing building across the street.

Mean colored lightning bolts flashed before Amanda Newton's eyes. A croquet ball size knot in her chest forced her to swallow the disco's stagnant, smoke filled air which was the result of one of Bo's ideas that backfired. He had wanted pyrotechnics to go with each of Obadiah's hog calls. Instead, he got a loud fizzing sound that preceded a single, tiny explosion that spit out a Roman candle sized projectile. The projectile was a bull's eye hitting the mirrored ball above the dance floor. Tiny mirrored squares rained down, most of them finding the end of the bar where Amanda Newton sat stewing and fine tuning her revenge. She was ready to unleash it on whomever the culprit was that interrupted her coffee break earlier. Adding spice to Amanda Newton's stew was an image of her being filmed with her backpack in compromising sexual positions.

Amanda tried to make sense of what had happened to her during her day off and the opportunity to savor MT. In a brief span of several hours, her bottom had been massaged by the grateful leather cushion of her stool and she had sipped her favorite, flavored coffee. Then there was a ghastly phone call followed by a traffic jam, rude parking attendants asking for an outrageous sum of money and comments coming from a mob that wadded up political correctness into an ugly ball and tossed it into a waste paper basket of garish language. One of those comments had forced her to unearth a long stored tactic of retaliation she had once learned from an aunt when she was about to enter womanhood. The aunt, a black sheep of Amanda's social register family for having a career in Roller Derby, had taught her the proper use of the human patella to correct those who didn't adhere to Emily Post's strict code on manners and the use of appropriate vocabulary. What caught her by surprise was finding herself being cordial to the man she hated more than anything else in the world. As tiny pieces of mirror bounced off her head and shoulders, she was wondering about her daughter's safety and having second thoughts about climbing over the bar to either strangle or hug her former spouse. All she managed to say to Sam after recovering from being flabbergasted was a chilly, "Yes, it has been a long time." As the last word of her greeting seeped out, she was overtaken by an additional thought and the increase in her heart rate. She wanted her ex-husband with a passion and to scream out, "Geronimo!"

Ben could have hugged Sam. The bartender's cordial greeting to Matilda's mother gave him time to make new plans for survival. Somehow, he was going to prevent his early demise at the hands of his girlfriend's angry mother. Then his plans hit a snag as he saw that his own mother noticed him. So did John Brown. "Oh, no," he muttered, his stomach coming under siege by a squadron of butterflies with the fangs of a marauding pack of starving hyenas. He could see that neither his mother nor the attorney possessed a single shred of happiness and warmth and he quickly reassessed his options. Smooth talk coated with outright falsehoods wouldn't be enough to add another day to his longevity. Panic and stomach cramps sent him on a bee line for the men's room.

Noel now found that he had another assignment at La Tinkerbelle's along with his being assistant maitre d' and head of security to protect Matilda Newton. Since answering Sam's urgent call for help, he had mixed drinks behind the bar, mashed potatoes in the kitchen and repaired two jammed projectors in the men's room. The last job took the longest since he wanted to be sure that the projectors ran properly. Now he was being jostled by the crowd and felt as if he were a human ping pong ball being bounced back and forth—all one hundred and thirty-five pounds of him. His bouncing stopped when he faced his grandmother and her party from Glen Forest on the

Watercourse. Noel's extensive training as a law enforcement professional had not prepared him for having to tell his grandmother that she had to pay a cover charge in order to be admitted into the discotheque. He swallowed, took a deep breath, smiled and said, "What a wonderful surprise, Grandma." He took a quick glance to either side. "There will be a small cover charge of ten dollars." He took another quick glance. "Are these lovely people with you?"

"These lovely people are my friends from Glen Forest on the Watercourse, Noel," his grandmother said. "I'm sure you've seen them in The Emporium sipping a latte when you visit me on Sundays."

Noel hadn't but he nodded anyway. He offered his arm to his grandmother and said, "Let me escort you and your friends."

Margaret, ever the thoughtful and polite one, stepped aside to let her friends in front of her and her grandson. There was a minimum of shoving mainly because of the breasts that belonged to Alice Nell Puffin, Linda Ann Finn and Principal Lucia Gunderson running interference. Noel escorted his grandmother and her group behind the maitre d' stand where Bo stood, still in a trance, as if he were at the helm of his ship. "Excuse me, Captain," he said politely to Bo, every pocket of his uniform stuffed with money. "My grandmother, her lady friends from Glen Forest on the Watercourse and the Reverend here," he nodded at a sweating, bug eyed Rufus Puffin who had seen the bandstand and couldn't wait to get to his new pulpit to save souls, "would appreciate being allowed to move up to the head of the line. Grandmother is up in years and waiting in long lines doesn't agree with her arthritis."

"Five dollars," Bo said, his eyes as black and lifeless as two pitted black olives.

Noel's grandmother turned to the others and said politely, "Cough up a buck each, ladies." She flicked her open palm in their direction. "And, that'll be a buck for you too, Rev."

CLICK/SNAP!

"Five dollars," Bo repeated, the two black olives glowing from a coating of extra virgin olive oil."

Noel's grandmother handed Bo five singles.

"Thank you," said Bo, tossing the five singles under his maitre'd stand. "Noel, take your dear, sweet grandmother to the bar. Sam will take care of her. Tell him I said to buy her a drink."

Noel smiled, nodded and took his grandmother by the hand, leaving her friends standing next to Bo at the maitre d' stand.

"Five dollars," said Bo, blocking the path of the others in the group from Glen Forest on the Watercourse.

"We just paid," lisped an annoyed Lucia Gunderson. "You took our money. I saw you." She pointed at the maitre'd stand. "You put it under there."

"Five dollars," repeated Bo, the black olives glistening even more.

Linda Ann Finn stepped in front of Lucia Gunderson. "Do you know who I am?" she asked Bo.

"Five dollars," said Bo, his voice like a nasal computerized recording.

"My husband is the Chief of Police of Glen Forest on the Watercourse," said Linda Ann, flashing her best authoritarian look and thrusting out her prominent breasts that were encased in an uplift bra she had selected for the trip. "I know you're a resident of Glen Forest on the Watercourse," she said, her breasts receiving an added oomph. "My husband could make living in our fair community so much easier for you." She inhaled even harder, her breasts making contact with Bo's sleeve as she moved her shoulders from right to left and back again.

"Five dollars," said Bo, his recorded message playing on cue.

"Excuse me, good soul," said Pastor Rufus Puffin, sweating more profusely that ever, his Bible getting the brunt. "Surely a man of the cloth and these fine Christian women should be exempt from paying a fee to be a witness to Satan's work."

"Five dollars," said Bo.

Alice Nell Puffin stepped politely in front of her husband, smiled at Bo, ran her tongue slowly over her upper lip and, like Linda Ann Finn inhaled, her air intake almost removing Bo's captain's hat from his head. Her breasts rested on the grateful edge of the maitre'd stand. "Are ya'll saying to us poor little ol' ladies from your home town that we have to pay five dollars each to come visit ya'll in your cute as a bug in a rug disco?" She smiled, her tongue now traveling across her lower lip and her breasts joining Linda Ann Finn's against Bo's sleeve. "Why, honey, you and me and my dear lady friends, Christian lady friends I might add, well, we're almost kinfolk." Her tongue journeyed across both lips with added flicks inserted. "Certainly four sweet ladies who have always admired you should be exempt from your silly old cover charge. That is what it is called when an establishment such as your serves the devil's brew, isn't it?" Her breasts thrust forward almost knocking Bo over. "And makes sinners pay for the privilege."

"Five dollars," said Bo.

Wanda Mensch stepped in front of Alice Nell Puffin. Unlike the pastor's wife and the other ladies in the group, she wore only a trace of lip stick and didn't bother to inhale. It wouldn't have mattered. She reached in her purse, pulled out a five dollar bill and handed it to Bo. "I was Mayor Bell's personal secretary and I understand the fundamentals of fiscal and financial management after working for him."

Bo seemed to come out of his trance and gave Wanda a polite nod. "It's refreshing to meet a lovely charming lady who understands how money provides the lubricant that makes an economic entity run smoothly." He gave her a slanted smile, his not as pronounced as Lucia Gunderson's, and stepped aside. He pointed in the direction of the bar. "Ask for Sam and tell him Captain Bo said, no, ordered, that he should give you whatever your heart desires." As Wanda walked by, Bo stepped in front of Lucia Gunderson, Linda Ann Finn, Alice Nell Puffin and Pastor Rufus Puffin. "Five Dollars," he said.

"Mandy," said Sam to his ex-wife. "Our little girl's in good hands. Do you think for one minute that I'd put her in harm's way?"

"Yes, I do think that," Amanda shot back. "She's here in this disgusting, garish place isn't she?" The flashing colors from the strobe lights raced across her eyes and caused her to squint. "Where is she? I'm taking her home this instant."

"I don't even know if our little girl is here," said Sam, leaning forward on his elbows. "If she is, I'm sure she's safe, secure and smiling," said Sam, as he politely slid a tall, ice filled glass in front of her. "When she's here she's always surrounded by loving, caring people who wouldn't let a single, solitary hair on her pretty head be harmed. Look around. All of those pirates you see on roller blades; the pirates you see working behind the bar and all the others. They're security. They're Chicago cops hired to protect the customers and all of us here, especially our Princess Matty." He gave the tall ice filled glass a gentle nudge in her direction. "Why don't you take a sip of the house specialty," he said softly, a reassurance in his voice. It's called, Windy City Iced Tea, my version of the Long Island stuff. Mine's better and I know you'll like it. I still remember your tastes."

"All I want is my daughter," she said, the angry flashing colors becoming subdued. She put the twin straws in the glass to her lips and took a sip of the drink. The man on the other side of the bar who was once her husband, the man who had crushed her spirit, did know her tastes.

"Our daughter is in good hands, Mandy."

"Our daughter?" asked Amanda, her crushed spirit stirring.

"She'll always be my princess."

Amanda sipped at her drink, her frustrations being taken out on a pair of straws by an angry thumb and index finger pinching the straws almost shut so her cheeks were slightly caved in. She looked at Sam and eased the tension in her fingers as the straws slipped from her sensuous lips. "How can you refer to my daughter as your princess?" she asked, the stirring spirit stretching and flexing its muscles. "Are you forgetting who walked out on who and walked away with that poor excuse of a Who?" She took another sip of her drink. "Now, you're permitting my little girl to be in this glorified saloon."

"Do you like?" Sam asked, referring to the drink and knowing when to change the topic of conversation.

"The drink, yes," replied Amanda. "This saloon, no," she concluded then almost sucking the bottom of the glass up through her straws.

Sam, not taking his eyes off Amanda, returned to making drinks, his hands working at a frenzied pace under the bar while he kept glancing at his ex-wife. He watched her take another sip of her Windy City Iced Tea. "Our Matty's fine," he said. He smiled and added, "If you're interested, the tea in your drink comes from Ceylon. I believe via Manhattan, the Bronx and Staten Island."

The straws slid their way out of her mouth. "Lines from one of my favorite songs," she said her words minus anger and her heart rate increasing again. The straws returned their path back to her lips. This time she took a dainty sip. She looked at Sam and saw something she had never noticed in him before. Peace. The straws slipped from her mouth. "You have a good memory."

"We listened to that song on our honeymoon," said Sam. "Remember?"

Amanda nodded her eyes downcast.

"Our honeymoon was good, wasn't it?" asked Sam.

Matilda stood on the steel grating of the aerialist's platform looking down on the inundating waves of human heads. She was becoming seasick and didn't know it, her new nausea climbing on board with her jangled nerves. Her mother still hadn't discovered her new career in the performing arts and the sideways deception associated with it. She started to cry. Adding to her woe were here fingers. They wouldn't cooperate with the buckles of her harness. "What am I going to do, girlfriends?" she asked Peter and Pan. "My mother thinks I'm performing in a play about Peter Pan. She has no idea I'm Tinker Bell in a leotard," she said, her entire body starting to tremble. "Would God punish me if I ran out the back door and never came back?"

"Nobody's going to punish you," said Peter giving her a reassuring hug.

"Peter's right," said Pan as she stepped in and also gave Matilda a hug.

Matilda tried to laugh, but nothing came out. "At least my father now knows," she said. "My boyfriend told me that his uncle convinced my father that I wanted to be in the show. I guess my father agreed." She glanced down at the packed, shouting and pushing crowd. "That's what I was told and I do pray the story is true."

"I'm sure it's true," said Peter. "Ben isn't the kind of kid who would lie. You have nothing to worry about, Matty." She took a glance down and then up. "And when those spotlights, along with that mirrored dance hall ball and the strobe lights blind your mother, you won't have a thing to worry about," Peter continued as she adjusted her own harness. "Your mother will never know who's behind that Tinker Bell mask."

Matilda inched closer to the edge of the platform and looked down. Her stomach dropped. She could see her mother sitting at the bar, both hands wrapped around a tall glass, talking to her father. "Oh, my God," muttered Matilda, fear coating each word. "My mother's talking to my father."

"Your mother and Sam?" blurted out Peter.

"Sam and your mother, the high school librarian?" asked Pan gripping at the steel rail of the platform to regain her balance. "Holy crap, your mother and Sam?" she asked.

"Our Sam and your mother?" asked Peter feeling her body go numb.

"That's definitely my mother at the bar talking to my father," said Matilda, backing slowly away from the edge of the platform. "And she's next to Ben's mother and that lawyer friend of hers who gives me the creeps."

"Ben's mother," they repeated in unison.

Matilda nodded. "Now do you understand why I asked if God would punish me if I ran away?"

Peter and Pan barely moved their heads up and down once and said in unison, "Sanctorum cacas."

Matilda started to giggle. "If my mother has her Alpine backpack with her, the one she always wears when she walks to school, I'm in trouble. She looks like a teeny bopper going on safari."

"She doesn't carry any kind of a dangerous weapon in there,

does she?" asked Pan, her harness buckles clicking shut.

"I don't think so," said Matilda. "I know she has a can of mace."

"Let's hope not," said Pan, adjusting her harness to keep it from pinching the inside of her thighs.

Matilda looked down again to see an elderly lady she didn't recognize standing next to Noel Jones who she did recognize. Then her knees started to shake. Next to Noel Jones was the late Mayor's secretary. She didn't know her name, but she knew the face, seeing it many times over the years living in the apartment above the mortuary. Her knees began to shake even more when she saw Pastor Puffin, his wife and the wife of the Chief of Police. Matilda Newton latched onto the right arm of Peter and the left arm of Pan. "I'm so glad you're my friends and that you understand," she said to them. "I'm ready," she said, taking a deep breath and stepping to the edge of the platform. She glanced left and right and saw reassuring nods and friendly smiles. Matilda shouted a word she thought she had heard as a little girl watching a western movie on television. Along with her two partners, she stepped off the platform screaming, "Geronimo!"

Neither of her parents looked up. They couldn't hear because of the pandemonium.

Bo, for the first time since being overwhelmed by the sight of a mob of paying customers, found himself fidgeting at the maitre d' stand. For one of the rare times in his life he got the feeling that money didn't matter to him. There was something else and that something else was gnawing on his very being. He kept turning and looking, his black eyes pleading as he searched the crowd waiting for Officer Noel Jones to return.

His searching lasted only a few seconds before he found himself reaching and grabbing a five dollar bill from an outstretched hand. Then there was a hundred dollar bill thrust in his face along with the request, "Hey, Horatio Hornblower, how 'bout four seats up front?"

Bo snatched the hundred dollar bill, held it up to the light mounted on his maitre d' stand then jammed it into his white, Captain's jacket pocket. "Right this way," he said, his hand ushering the four customers in front of him into the crowd. He gave the last one in the group a hard shove and the four were swallowed up by the throng. Bo turned back to his position at the maitre d' stand and jumped. Someone had grabbed his shoulder from behind.

It was Noel Jones. The diminutive, almost effeminate door man, undercover cop, bouncer and the holder of every colored belt the Marshall arts awarded was with his grandmother. "We were at the bar and Sam took care of my grandmother. After her drink, she insisted on coming back here to talk. She had never met a real captain before."

Mildred Farnsworth Pepperwall Jones smiled at Bo and asked, "Are you really a captain? Do you really steer ships and sing about sixteen men on a dead man's chest and drink rations of grog?"

Bo nodded.

"I had an ancestor who was a General in the army during the Revolutionary War," she said proudly. "He was the founder of Glen Forest on the Watercourse, our beloved, prestige community. Did you know that, Captain?"

Bo snapped to attention and saluted Noel's grandmother. "Aye, indeed I did," replied Bo, having minimal knowledge of the shenanigans of General Glen Forest Pepperwall. "No finer a town founder have I heard in all my years at the helm of this fine vessel flying the Jolly Roger," he lied. He looked at Noel's grandmother and asked, "How would you like to take the wheel of this magnificent vessel and find a night star that will guide us over these here treacherous seas to the bandstand?"

"Really?" asked Mildred Farnsworth Pepperwall Jones.

Bo smiled and nodded.

"Oh, my," said Noel's grandmother. "I'm honored."

"And so you should be," said Bo, striking up a pose that wouldn't be out of place in Trafalgar Square. "Madam," he stated gazing into her eyes, "I must go down to the sea again, to the lonely sea and the sky; and all I ask is a tall ship and a star to steer her by." His eyes accompanied his poetry. "Dear lady, since Mr. Masefield isn't available, would you be my star?"

Mildred's entire face lit up brighter than the spotlights illuminating the trio streaking across the ceiling. She had never been on a ship let alone steer one. "Do you really lash mutinous sailors with a cat 'o nine tails?"

"Aye," replied Bo. "But only those who don't pay their five dollars for the privilege of sailing with me," he said waving his hand over the crowd as if he were giving a Papal blessing. "When you're at the helm and someone wants to get by you it will cost them…."

"Five dollars," she interrupted, repeating. "I remember."

"A good memory like yours will take you far on these pirate infested waters," Bo said to her. He watched Noel's grandmother snatch a bill, thank the patron and stuff the bill in the bodice of her dress without making change.

"Next," said Noel's grandmother.

Bo flipped a couple of bills he had in each hand under the maitre d' stand not seeming to care where they landed. He glanced at Noel's grandmother approvingly then gave Noel a serious look. "May I ask you a legal question?" he said to the undercover cop while Mildred continued grabbing at money and shouting out, "Next!"

"Ask away," said Noel, looking up at Bo and feeling as if he had been punched in the stomach by his boss's look. "You're the Captain. Or, as we used to say when I was in the Marines and stationed at the Atsugi Naval Air Station in Japan, the Ichi-ban Honcho."

"I don't have any itches," said Bo, swallowing hard and not stopping. "If a guy saw a crime committed, would he be guilty if he didn't tell the police?"

"What kind of crime?" asked Noel?

Bo stared straight ahead as if in a trance. "Murder," he stated, the computerized voice gone.

"Perhaps we should talk in private when you get a chance," replied Noel, trying not to show that Bo's question did, indeed, knock the wind out of him.

"One other question," said Bo, his head looking toward the bar. "Do you know anything about that one lady standing at the end of the bar with that group from the village?"

"Which lady is that?" repeated Noel Jones. The only lady I know here besides my grandmother is your sister, The Mayor.

Bo smiled, his mustache changing directions of its slant and he pointed in the direction where Wanda Mensch was standing and said, "The one who worked for my late brother-in-law and now for my sister."

"I think her name's Wanda. Wanda Mensch," said Noel.

"My grandmother introduced us. Gram knows everyone both living and dead in that community of yours," continued Noel. "She's always trying to introduce me to women, wants to marry me off."

"You're not going to are you?" said Bo, still looking toward the bar.

"Marry Wanda Mensch?" stated Noel, his answer joined by a sheepish grin. "Nah," he said with a blush. "No marriage for me. I'm not the marrying kind."

"Good," said Bo.

SNAP/CLICK! SNAP/CLICK! SNAP/CLICK!

Reggie, Rommie and Regis were beyond elated. In their sixty plus years as musicians they had never played before a crowd the size that packed La Tinkerbelle's. "Man, dig those clams," hollered Reggie to his two partners.

"Never seen so many cats and kittens at one gig ever," replied Rommie.

"Enough with the chin jive, gents," said Reggie. "It's time to jam." He dabbed at his runny nose with the top of a lace handkerchief he took from the pocket of his red and black plaid tuxedo jacket and returned it, the cardboard bottom half of the handkerchief getting stuck and bending as it went back into his pocket.

Bo left a befuddled Noel working alongside his grandmother collecting cover charges. He slid through tiny gaps in between the crush of humanity by turning his shoulders sideways and, with a dipping-pushing-lunging motion, sans goosing, sent alcoholic beverages splashing from the glasses. "Sorry," he kept apologizing, knowing that he really wasn't sorry that he had caused the people in his way to spill their drinks. Spilled drinks meant refilled drinks and refilled drinks meant more money in his pockets.

He stopped and stood alongside of Wanda Mensch. "Excuse me, Miss Mensch," he said, in his most polite, dignified manner. "I'd like to formally introduce myself. I'm Berthold Pepperwall owner of La Tinkerbelle's a Go-Go."

Wanda smiled, felt her knees feel the way they did after she would leave Mildred's Ennui Latte Emporium after sipping Gentleman Jack with the owner well into a Sunday evening.

"Sam," Bo called out getting his bartender's attention. He held up his the index finger of his right hand. "Take care of Miss Mensch's imbibing needs," he shouted out. He paused for a minute looking perplexed then said: "Put this on my tab."

"Miss Mensch," said Sam, ever the efficient bartender as he made his way to the end of the bar. "I believe your drink is a Gentleman Jack neat, is it not?"

Wanda Mensch smiled at Sam and asked in a quiet, sheepish voice: "Would it be proper for me to switch to a glass of

Dandelion wine?"

"Dandelion wine it is," said Sam. He smiled and didn't miss a beat. His hand found a chilled bottle of open Chardonnay and he poured it into a wine glass. Then he added several splashes each of Ouzo and Sambucca. There was a quick stir from a swizzle stick, a garnish of fresh Rosemary and he handed the glass to Wanda. "Dandelion wine ala La Tinkerbelle's," he said. "Enjoy. It's our special house blend." He smiled and added. "And, it is very proper indeed."

Bo smiled at Wanda his smile looking like puppy love and Wanda smiled the same smile back. Then Bo gave Amanda's bar stool a gentle push to the side and squeezed up to bar. He smiled meekly at Wanda, turned, all traces of a smile gone and said to Sam: "What are we going to do?"

"Do," echoed Sam carefully?

"The crowd," said Bo, his head cocked back toward the customers crushed up against the bar. "Do you think they read the paper?"

Sam shot Bo a look that said, "Of course they read it, Boss. That's why they're here."

"Great," said Bo, sounding disgusted. "Just great," he continued. "Now we're going to have to give them a wedding."

"A wedding," repeated Sam, his hands coming to a standstill.

The straws to Amanda Newton's drink slipped from her mouth with a slurp. "Did you say a wedding?"

"A wedding," repeated Wanda. "Did you say a wedding?"

"That I did," said Bo. "That Izzy Inman's article said there would be a wedding here today and, as captain of this pirate ship, I'm legally entitled to marry any one aboard. Noel told me that. He glanced at Wanda. "I could even marry you, Miss Mensch," he said, then turned his attention to Sam and didn't notice half the dandelion wine being absorbed by Wanda's blouse. "I could even marry you, Sam and you're my very best friend in the whole world."

Amanda inhaled so hard she sucked the straws half way out of her drink making slurping sounds like the kids used to during World War II in Shakes when it was a malt shop.

Bo smiled at Amanda Newton. "If you don't want to marry my very best friend in the whole world, then you can be a flower girl for whoever I pronounce my nautical nuptial blessings on."

"A flower girl," repeated Amanda, the numbing pain from the temporary brain freeze she got from the icy drink clearing her head.

"Of course," said Bo. "If you think you want a higher rank, I'll make you a maid of honor. If he wants, Sam can be your escort. A more handsome groomsman a shipboard wedding has ever seen."

"You want Sam and me in a saloon wedding?" Amanda asked, her brain freeze gone but the rest of her body feeling like Lake Michigan in February.

Sam tried not to grin. "The Captain is not making you walk the plank," he said to Amanda. "This is all business to him," he continued. "The newspaper said wedding and Bo wants to provide what Izzy Inman advertised. You'll never find a more honest business man than Bo." Sam paused, smiled and said, "A bit of a conniver, but an honest, harmless conniver and a heart bigger than the ocean his La Tinkerbelle sails on."

CLICK/SNAP!

"I'll marry Obadiah and Emerine," said Bo matter-of-factly. "It wouldn't be a lie since they're common law spouses."

CLICK/SNAP!

Amanda Newton inched her empty glass in Sam's direction. "I think I need another one of these," she said, a blank look on her cover girl model's face. "Sam," she said, her eyes pleading, "Promise me that my little girl is safe."

Obadiah launched himself on the bandstand with a one hand vault kicking the boombass out of Regis's hand. It crashed against the microphone stand filling the club with an ear splitting, hissing static that made faces cringe and teeth grind. "Sorry, Mr. Regis," said Obadiah. His thick southern drawl apology sounded like it had been filtered through a work boot filled with cheese grits. He tapped the microphone and heard the deafening echo. "Attention," he shouted, waiting for the quiet that didn't come. "Attention!" he shouted again. The crowd ignored him. "Hey, man, how about some attention," he pleaded. He gave his shoulders a shrug, removed the microphone from the chrome stand and shouted: "Sueeey, Pig! Yaaa! Sueeey! Hog!" If a hand was free it shot up to seal off an ear. Obadiah glanced at Rommie whose long, crooked arthritic fingers rested on the neck of his guitar. Reggie opened and closed the bellows of his Dick Contino autographed accordion while Regis gave his boombass a couple of test taps against the bandstand floor.

"Thank ya'll," said Obadiah, making the three words a single syllable. He stepped quickly to the edge of the bandstand and held out his hand. Emerine, tambourine in her left hand, reached out with her right and Obadiah pulled her up as if she were a rag doll to join him.

"They're doin' it," came a single cry from the packed discotheque. Izzy Inman's readers surged toward the bandstand like a tidal wave of molasses. The crowded boutique emptied so fast Frank and Charles felt as if they had been sucked into a vacuum. Even the waiters and waitresses stopped skating to look.

Obadiah grinned at the crowd, put his arm around Emerine's ample waist and cut loose with another championship hog call.

Bo's captain's uniform now appeared neat and somehow his trousers appeared creased and the jacket buttons in line thanks to the efficient fingers of Wanda Mensch. He strutted toward the bandstand with Wanda in tow.

Wanda had never known a captain before, only a Mayor, and this set off a new series of fantasies pulsating through her. "Grab hold of my collar and don't let go," she heard Bo say to her, his reassuring words ordering her to grab excited her even more. Bo discarded his strut turning himself into a human wedge. He began to plow his way from the bar area to the band stand, Wanda hanging onto his collar almost choking him as she was being drug behind him. He climbed up on the bandstand then bent down, put his hands under tiny Wanda's arm pits and lifter her to the stage like a feather. The crowd cheered. In his left hand Bo held what appeared to be a Bible. In a way it was.

It was a red bound copy of the Bartender's Bible that Sam kept under the bar along with his homemade blackjack.

Bo didn't need a spotlight. He glowed like the beam from the searchlight truck he had hired for his charity gala several weeks earlier. The mob turned silent as the lights went black. Hans, who had left the gate house after a frantic phone call from Bo to moonlight, had flipped the master switch located on the wall behind the launch platform that Tinker Bell, Peter and Pan used. The switch controlled the disco's flashing lights, the mirrored ball and blinking, strobe light beams. Bo cleared his throat into the microphone. There was no sound. He tapped the microphone, again no sound. He looked at the band members and Reggie, Regis and Rommie all attacked the amplifier at once. There was still no sound. Then Bo gave a silent Hiel, Hitler salute. Hans clicked his heels and jammed his index finger into the control box so hard he cracked the power button in three places. Bo coughed into the microphone again and free hands sought ears. Bo smiled, almost leered. "Hello, Chicago," he stated, as if he were the lead singer in a cheap, one night stand rock group giving a concert. He savored the applause, whistles and howls that followed not bothering to put his hands up in a gesture of asking for quiet. He didn't want quiet. "Ladies and gentlemen," he announced, holding up a folded newspaper. "What all of you read in this morning's paper, a column by the one and only Chicagoan in the know, Izzy Inman, is gospel." The crowd erupted. Bo smiled and signaled for quiet and waited. When he got it he held up a rolled newspaper which was nothing more than a price leader ad for a local supermarket chain. Izzy Inman's column was somewhere on the floor of Bo's office. "If it's a wedding you came to see, it's a wedding you're going to get. La Tinkerbelle's a Go-Go, the world's most famous discotheque of all time, stands and delivers."

Regis, Reggie and Rommie began to play the soft strains of, *The Theme from Love Boat.*

Wanda Mensch's tiny hands clasped together and rested in the area of her heart.

Craning necks, people jumping up and down in front of her window and women being hoisted onto men's shoulders caught Captain Hookette's attention. It dawned on her that no one was looking at her. "What's going on?" she thought. She held up her phallic shaped hook, gripped it in her right hand and waved it in front of the window. "Hey, perverts," she hollered as the rubber hook danced back and forth. "Wanna go for a ride on the good ship Venus?"

No one noticed. No one heard. No one cared. The jockeying for a better position to see what they were trying to see continued in front of her. "Oh, for heaven's sake," she said, an annoyed frustration in her voice. She stopped waving the rubber phallic symbol hook, dropped it to the floor of her glass enclosed stage, pulled the curtain shut and exited out her tiny entrance door bumping her shin and tearing one of her veils in the process. "Ouch. Damn."

Naomi Schmitt started inching her way through the crowd

that was packed so tight together it looked like a single person with the widest set of shoulders ever created. "Excuse me," she said, with each gentle nudge forward, the shoulders barely budging. Three nudges and steps later she was minus two veils. Another step had her saying, "Move it, lard bottom." The next step saw her punching an anonymous patron in the nuts for grabbing at her spangled bra. Then she saw Noel summoning her at the maitre d' stand just as the crowd began chanting: "We want a wedding!"

The chanting grew more raucous, even nasty, the crowd substituting for what they wanted instead of a wedding. That didn't deter Bo. The glow emanated from him seemed to increase in brilliance. He held up his hands for silence, but once again the crowd ignored him, some of them changing their chant to: "Rip off! Rip off! Rip off!"

Bo, hands and arms outstretched, gave a series of nods. The first went to the band. The second was cast up to the metal platform at the top of the club and the third nod was back to the band.

Regis, Rommie and Reggie knew what to do. So did Obadiah. He grabbed the microphone from Bo, turned the volume up on the amplifier to full blast and let out another one of his championship hog calls. It was a pure blue ribbon effort. Red faced, he grabbed a stone faced Emerine Randall by the hand and pulled her to him just as the band started playing, "Come Fly With Me."

Over head, Tinker Bell, Peter and Pan launched themselves from the platform after having taken a rest break. They soared back and forth across the cavernous ceiling area, Matilda enjoying the calm she felt after once again shouting out,

"Geronimo." With the ceiling lights out, thanks to Hans, the audience hadn't heard or noticed them. That's when Bo grabbed the microphone from Obadiah and shouted, "Look; up in the sky. It's a bird! It's a plane. No!" Bo gasped for breath and shouted, "It's Peter, Pan and, oh my goodness gracious great balls of fire, it's Tinker Bell!" He looked up and saw black. Bo quickly put the microphone next to his mouth and shouted: "Hans, Hiel, Hitler you stupid Nazi twit. Turn on the lights." Nothing happened. Then Bo shouted, "Dumbkopf, the search lights! Americano planes!" As if by the hand of God, black turned to a starlit blue, the mirrored ball glistened and the strobe lights shot their flashing beams over head. There were hushed murmurs of assorted awes heard around the club as heads looked up. Then screaming, cheering and yelling erupted.

Frank saw the sequined trio as he cautiously emerged from the boutique. "Chuckie Charles, you sad, sick homo, get over here and feast your beady eyes on our lovely sisters," he said knowing the name, Chuckie would irritate his partner. He pointed up.

Charles got up off the floor, brushed at his sleeves that had almost been torn from his shirt, gave a nip, tuck and primp and then headed to Frank. "What now, Willie Wonka Wolfman with the curdled creamy center?" He glared at Frank and said, "You know how I hate being called Chuckie." Then his eyes followed the direction that Frank's head was pointing. He exhaled, fought back a tear and said: "Oh, my, our sisters are exquisite." He sighed, reached for Frank's hand and stated: "Aren't they adorable."

At the bar, all Sam noticed in between pouring drinks were

three black sequined shapes streaking in an arc across the ceiling of the foundry. Sweat was burning his eyes as he concentrated on not spilling a drop.

Sweat wasn't burning the eyes of Amanda Newton or making her vision blurry. Sam's Windy City Iced Teas had done that. The drinks didn't, however, prevent a mother from thinking she recognized her daughter, no matter how many sequins covered her and no matter how protected she was by a glittered mask. She jumped off her bar stool, spilled her drink, felt a combination of being dizzy and nauseous and tried to catch her balance.

Just as the soaring trio made another pass over the crowd, a patron in front of the stage cupped his hands to his mouth and shouted, "Hey, where's the Money Mad Miz and the Christian Crier!"

A second patron standing in front of the stage watched his shirt soak up half of his drink, his tie soaking up almost the other half. He squinted at Emerine Randall and shouted: "Hey, grandma, you ain't the Money Mad Miz!"

"She's up there," yelled back Emerine, pointing to the trio racing across the ceiling. "It don't take no college education to figure that out, you dumb ass Yankee."

The crowd let out a gasp. Just then, Pan, her harness pinching her crotch, reached down and tried to adjust it. After several pulls and tugs she yelled out another, "Geronimo!"

"Geronimo," repeated Peter feeling giddy. She waved at the crowd below and started blowing kisses.

Matilda's arms were out in front of her as if she were playing Superwoman. The elastic band holding her black sequined mask in place was fastened so tight she felt dizzy. Her head once buried between her arms in an effort to conceal her identity now stood out proud.

Amanda Newton bent forward, placed her straws in her mouth, the other ends in the puddle on the bar that had been her drink and began making slurping sounds. When her slurping stopped she bent back and stared up at the ceiling squinting and trying to clear her vision.

Arvia tried looking up at the trio, but the strobe lights blinded her.

"Wow," yelled John Brown as he licked his lips. "Look at the rack on that hot little broad in the middle." He slid his empty martini glass toward the edge of the bar and said what he shouldn't have said to Sam: "Hit me."

Ben, who had found a temporary sanctuary outside the girls' dressing room, caught glimpses of the go-go girls in the six cages and snippets of Matilda and Peter and Pan appearing before, after and between the cages as they continued sweeping across the ceiling of the club. Then his eyes traveled to the end of the bar where he could make out Matilda's mother, his mother and John Brown. Both mothers were squinting. John Brown wasn't moving. His head was resting on the bar, his right cheek up, his left cheek hidden against the top of the bar. A severe bruise was concealed by the bar. Ben's heart sank even further when he recognized the new school principal, the Police Chief's wife and who he knew was the Pastor of the United Church of the Glen's wife. Everyone in the high school and country day school knew of Alice Nell Puffin. Ben could see their heads looking up, eyes straining as they tried to focus on the show going on above. Ben focused on Sam and felt relief. Sam was working. Then he shifted his sights on his uncle on the bandstand. He took a second look to make sure he saw what he thought he saw; his mother's secretary was standing next to his uncle, her arm looped through the arm opposite the one holding a red book. He watched his uncle, the pastor and Obadiah who appeared to be in a three way pulling match with the microphone and the red Bible. Then he heard a screech from the speakers that made his eyes cross.

Reggie, Rommie and Regis hadn't missed a beat. They went from *Over the Bounding Main* into the *Banana Boat Song.* Obadiah let out another hog call, this one subdued because Bo had snatched the microphone from him and stuffed it inside the front of his Captain's jacket to keep it away from the vocalist and Pastor Puffin. The sound of Bo's heart beating came over the speaker system, a perfect amplified tempo accompanying the Banana Boat Song.

As the trio of aerialists started another arc back above the floor, Amanda Newton continued to squint. Arvia sighed and saw her short political career coming to an abrupt, embarrassing end.

John Brown lay out cold on the bar. Sam had met the attorney's request by serving him his heavy, taped electrical cable instead of a Bombay Sapphire martini. The last words the lawyer heard came from Arvia who said, "Watch your filthy tongue." She had taken her eyes off the attorney for an instant to set her champagne flute down on the bar. Before her intended glare could find its target again, she saw John Brown face down and Sam appearing to be working, his hands out of sight under the bar.

Sam replaced his *Persuader*, one of many pet names he used to describe the weapon, put it in its secure hiding place and caught the attention of two of his waiters. They roller skated up to the bar and, without a word, each took an arm of the attorney and roller skated him to the back of the club sitting him propped up on the floor next to the fire escape door.

Thank you, Sam," said Arvia, toasting him with her champagne flute.

"I never thought I'd ever say this to you again, but, thank you, Sam," said Amanda. "That lawyer person is a disgusting excuse for a human being." She used the knuckles of her index fingers to brush away the tears. Squinting she looked up about the time Tinker Bell, Peter and Pan zipped directly over her. "Oh, my God," she said almost gouging out her eyes as the trio whizzed by. "My, God, Sam, it's our little girl!"

Ben, standing on the second step of the spiral stairs leading to the launching platform so he could get a better view, shifted his focus from the bandstand to see Matilda's mother get up from her seat at the bar, point her finger at Sam, turn and start pushing her way through the crowd to where he stood. "Oh, oh," he muttered.

Had Ben known that Amanda Newton had no interest in terminating his young life, his decision making process would have been different. He could see that Matilda's mother appeared to be on a mission and he was convinced he was a part of that mission. "Mrs. Newton, wait!" shouted Ben, as Matilda's mother pushed him aside and started up the winding metal stairs. She had knocked him off the second stair and he lay sitting on his backside watching her stumble up the stairs. "Mrs. Newton!" His words were swallowed up by the bedlam. He got up and started after his girlfriend's mother.

Sam did a one hand vault over the bar grabbing Arvia by the

arm before his feet hit the floor. "Come on, Your Honor," he said trying to pull her through the mob. His grip tightened as he led the way, plowing ahead toward the fire exit door. Both of them attempted to spot Ben and Amanda. Their attempts only turned up the unconscious figure of John Brown propped up against the wall next to the fire exit door. Sam looked at Arvia and said, "That lame brain brother of yours promised me my princess wouldn't be a part of his zany ideas. He swore to me that her part in his show would be dignified." He pointed up. "Look at the dignity. Do you see any dignity?"

Arvia said nothing. Then she saw her son and Matilda's mother, he was following her up the spiral staircase. "There," she said, pointing.

Sam's grip tightened even more on Arvia's arm until she yanked back and yelled out, "Sam, you're hurting me."

"Sorry," said Sam, his grip not loosening up. "We've got to catch them before there's trouble."

They made it to the top of the spiral staircase standing on the landing, both out of breath. Sam loosened his grip and Arvia rubbed at her arm. Neither of them took their eyes off of a son who was about to die and a mother who was about to kill her daughter. "Did you know about this, Ben?" asked Sam.

Ben knew he shouldn't say a word, but did. "She's Tinker Bell, Mister Sam, named after the character from Peter Pan. She's living her dream." He paused as the three adults looked at him if he had just climbed down from the rigging of the real Captain Hook's vessel. "And, if you bothered to look, she's not indecent, she's not lewd, she's only wearing a dancer's leotard and she's happy. She's really happy."

"Happy," shouted Amanda Newton. "You call that happy?"

She was pointing at the trio suspended from cables nearing the platform.

"Yes, Mam," he said politely. "I know she's happy. She told me."

Sam looked at Ben and then at his former wife. "You knew about all of this?" he asked.

Ben gave a single nod. "Yes, Sir," he said meekly.

Benoni, you knew?" The question came from a duet of two mothers who did not sound pleased; two sets of eyes were minus any signs of motherly love.

Ben nodded, his eyes downcast, his dreams of being a bass player in a rock band vaporizing along with his life.

"Mandy," said Sam, his head went from side to side. "I didn't know Bo's idea would be like this."

"You say my little girl is happy," said Amanda her words barely audible. "My little girl is happy?" she repeated. Her eyes traveled from Sam to Arvia to Ben and then back again. Then she screamed: "Well gosh dang it all to Hades, I'm not happy!"

Ben jumped.

Arvia jumped.

Sam stepped back until he felt the hand railing of the spiral staircase platform pressing against the top of his buttocks.

"Get her down!" Amanda shouted. "Do you hear me? Get her down from there!" A glow of red covered Amanda's face as she inhaled and then screamed out her order. "Get my baby down from there. NOW!"

"Oh, boy," said Ben. He looked at Sam and his mother. "Oh, boy," he repeated.

"Ben, get your uncle," ordered Arvia. She looked at Sam.

"But...," Ben managed to say.

"Now!" screamed his mother.

Bo, microphone in one hand and the Bartender's Bible in the other, asked the crowd: "How would you like to fly with those three?" His question was filled with static. "The holder of our lucky number will do just that."

"Fly, fly, fly!" the crowd began chanting, while all heads looked up at the three black clad characters in sequins soaring over them. Catcalls, whistles, and cheers for the trio were deafening.

Ben put his head down and tried bulldozing his way through the crowd in an effort to get to the bandstand. His efforts were more to save his life than to warn his uncle. Suddenly, he changed his mind, spun around and headed back towards the staircase at the back of the club.

Amanda Newton, operating on conflicting doses of alcohol, caffeine from her flavored coffee earlier and the adrenalin that rushed through her after Bo's phone call, heard the word at the same time as did Sam and Arvia. The three turned to come face-to-face with Hans.

"Achtung!" said Hans again, arms folded across his chest, a black neck tie tucked inside the front of his brown shirt.

"What?" said Amanda, taking a step toward Hans. "Did the Boy Scouts send you up here?"

"Verboten," said Hans, attempting to carry out another of the odd jobs that Bo had assigned to him. "You are not allowed up here," he said, scolding them then stomping the metal grating with the leather heals of his highly polished brown boots, the tops touching the bottoms of his matching brown jodhpurs. He took a single goose step to the edge of the platform.

"Don't tell me what I can and can't do, Buster Brown," said Amanda, shoving Hans in the chest as hard as she could and pushing him backwards.

"Sheisse," uttered a startled Hans. He had always relied on his two dogs, Schickle and Gruber to guard him. Now he found himself falling off the platform. A frantic, panicked grab of his right hand saw him hanging from the railing, his feet kicking at air. Then, remembering he was once a physical fitness trainer for a German health club, he used his swinging momentum to propel him back on the platform. He was furious. "Fraulein," he screamed at Amanda as he steadied himself on the platform. "Verdammt, hauen Sie ab!"

Sam heard what Hans said but the only word he understood was Fraulein. Had he possessed his taped electrical wire persuader, Hans would have been in a heap along side of John Brown at the Fire Exit door for telling his former wife to, "Get the fuck out of here."

"Mandy's going to be okay," said Sam, trying to do the impossible--keep two agitated mothers from killing their children after one of them had just tried to kill Hans. Sam looked at who he thought resembled a World War II German Gestapo member he had seen in movies blocking their path.

"Hans," said an astonished Arvia. "What are you doing

here?"

"Fraulein Arvia," he said, clicking his heels together. "Herr Bo hired me to protect the girls before, during and after their performances. I'm their body guard."

Arvia looked at the gate house guard. "Am I to assume that Schickle and Gruber our looking out after Dogwood?"

Hans smiled and nodded. "Your Dogwood is safe. Herr Bo has given me strict orders not to allow anyone up here. My orders are to keep the girls safe at all costs," he said spitting out his duties. "He's also put me in charge of the control box that raises and lowers the cages and keeps the wires separated so the young ladies won't get tangled." He held up the small rectangular control panel with a series of five black buttons. "Mien grobvater, as a teenager in Germany, used to operate a control system similar to this when he worked at a Krupp plant during the war."

Just then the trio of aerialists headed for the platform in a swinging arc. "Matilda!" screamed Amanda, trying to push aside Hans. "Young lady, you get down from there this moment."

Matilda saw her mother and went limp. Then, feeling a sense of bravado, she resumed her pose as a flying Tinker Bell that would have made Kathy Rigby proud.

"Matilda!" shouted Amanda Newton at her daughter. "Get down from there this instant." She tried to push her way to the edge of the platform but Hans held his ground. "Out of my way you Aryan imbecile," she said, and then punched Hans in the balls.

The proud sentry, protector of his girls as he called them, heard a whoosh. Then he felt agony. When he realized it had been the sound of his breath reluctantly fleeing from his lungs in a panic he knew exactly why his groin hurt. There was a look of surprise on his face after Amanda Newton's well aimed punch and he started to say, "Deutschland." He never got out, "uber alles" before he doubled up, kneeling on the platform as if in devout prayer.

Amanda latched onto the control panel hanging from a black cable about as round as Sam's homemade blackjack. Sam and Arvia stepped over Hans who was trying to gasp out, "verboten." Then they saw Matilda and her two companions soaring back in their direction. Amanda reached for her daughter but Matilda was too far away. The librarian lost her balance and, if it weren't for Sam's quick grab, she would've have fallen off the platform.

Matilda waved at her mother, smiled and shouted: "I'm alive!" Then she headed out over the crowd again, her flying Tinker Bell pose accentuated.

Frustrated, Amanda started pushing at the row of black buttons on the control unit.

Mandy, don't," warned Sam, trying to wrestle the unit from his ex-wife. His warning came too late as the hoist began to hum and started rolling slowly toward the platform.

Amanda wrestled to keep the control box away from Sam as Arvia and Ben stood and watched while Hans checked to see that he still had two of what he used to have. Amanda's thumb pushed down on a button just as Sam got the box away from her. Still fighting like a banshee, she squeezed Sam's hand forcing three of his fingers thrusting into an equal number of buttons on the panel. The motor and hoist appeared to leap and jump on its rail mounting.

The suspended cages below with the dancing go-go girls began to slowly rise up while the trio of aerialists continued to swing their cables getting shorter. The antiquated hoist motor whirled; sounds that the motor never experienced coughed from it. Up crept the six cages and closer came the hoist with the three aerialists attached. None of the performers dancing in the six cages knew what was going on above them.

About that time, Ben and his mother turned to see Alice Nell Puffin, Linda Ann Finn and Lucia Gunderson coming up the winding stairs. "I don't believe this is happening," said Ben, doing a double take and then seeing Matilda, Peter and Pan flying straight for the platform in a collision course. He could feel the platform vibrate and shake form the increased weight of the three newcomers at the top.

"Matilda Newton," said Amanda, the picture of a stern parent ready to reprimand a disobedient child. Her right index was thrust in the direction of her daughter. "You get over here this instant." Seeing her order ignored, she lunged making a desperate grab for her daughter. She misjudged the end of the arc, reached out and caught Peter instead. Before she could let lose, she felt herself being pulled off the platform. "Oh, poop," she gasped, feeling herself slide down Peter's body, the body parts slowly changing until she had latched onto Peter's thigh high, black, vinyl boots, her hands and arms clinging in a death grip to Peter's feet. A wing from each heal stuck out from between the fingers of both hands. Out she soared over the crowd.

The raucous crowd below cheered louder.

Pastor Puffin had wrestled the microphone away from Bo and was determined to marry Obadiah and Emerine in a proper religious ceremony. Bo backed away from Pastor Puffin who was swinging the microphone like the late General Pepperwall once lashed out with his saber in retreat. Any marriage, Bo thought, would appease the crowd and make him an even wealthier man. Both he and Pastor Puffin, Bibles in hand, were oblivious to what was going on over their heads.

Noel Jones wasn't. His emergency call was being spoken into the radio transmitter in his shirt pocket.

Suddenly, Bo looked up and saw the catastrophe unfolding above him. "Oh, shit," he muttered. Trouble was about to rain down on the crowd and he had to prevent that from happening. He bolted from the band stand taking Wanda Mensch with him. He shoved his way in the direction of the fire exit door and the spiral staircase. At the fire exit door he and Wanda saw John Brown's body propped up off to the side, the lawyer not moving. "He's evil," said Wanda gripping Bo's hand tighter. Bo pulled Wanda to the stairs, the two of them racing up the spiral metal steps where they saw Hans kneeling on all fours surrounded by Sam and four women. He stopped, looked at Hans and said, "I thought I told you to guard the young ladies and keep them safe."

Hans pointed at Amanda Newton who, a look of abject fear plastered across her model's face, was suspended from the ceiling in the middle of an arc hanging on to Peter's legs. "Der Fraulein punched me in die Hoden," he said.

Ben shifted forward on the platform and saw his mother. He had the hand railing in a choke hold as he reached out with his other hand for his girlfriend's mother. She was too far from him. Sam was behind Arvia, one arm looped through the vertical railing support and both of his hands clutched around her waist. As the swinging quartet neared the platform again, Arvia reached out for Amanda Newton. She misjudged the arc that has increased in speed with the shortening of the cable and came up with Amanda's blouse in her hand. The four women arced back out over the crowd.

Izzy Inman was caught in a massive traffic jam a block from La Tinkerbelle's and knew he was missing an important story. His nose was beginning to bleed and that omen told him that there was more than a story taking place at the discotheque. He heard his driver, Achmed lay on the horn. The cab that Izzy leased with Achmed as his driver didn't move. Izzy's bleeding nose did, the blood running freely. This was a story he couldn't miss. Had he witnessed what had already taken place at La Tinkerbelle's he would've been in his glory seeing the crowd and being able to join the wedding he had predicted. Had he been seated at the end of the bar at La Tinkerbelle's with his glass of Chartreuse he might have needed a transfusion when the crowd began shouting: "Take it off. Take it off. Take it all off," while Regis, Reggie and Rommie played, "The Stripper."

"Charge, Achmed!" ordered Izzy.

"Pronto, Tonto," replied Achmed using his two word English vocabulary that he knew his boss liked.

Pastor Puffin, witnessing what he believed was a sign from God going on above him, shouted into the microphone, "Sinners! Repent! The time is near!" Sweat cascaded down his forehead burning his eyes and making them redder than ever. His vision was blurred as the sweat continued along the rolls of his neck to be absorbed by his white clerical collar that was now stained yellow. "Repent!" he yelled again, his Scottish accent reaching into the depths of Hell to carry his message.

Obadiah and Emerine dropped to their knees. Arms outstretched they yelled out, "Alleluia!" The crowd didn't hear them and continued to chant, "Take it off!"

Arvia looked at Amanda Newton's blouse then saw the four women arcing back at a faster rate of speed while the six cages continue to inch upward, the go-go girls now realizing that this wasn't a part of their routine. Normally they would be going down. They heard Reggie, Rommie and Regis swing into their version of, "Fly Me to the Moon."

Tinker Bell, Peter and Pan realized they had picked up speed because of the added weight of Amanda Newton. Their screaming for help was now added by panic as they neared the platform along with the six rising cages. The go-go dancers hearing the four cries for help decided that screaming was the prudent thing to do. Noticing the thick cables scratching across the bars of their cages aided to being prudent.

Arvia reached out again for Amanda. She missed, slipped,

her weight jerking her out of Sam's grip and ended up clinging to Matilda's legs, one of her legs wrapped around the cable suspending Peter, the other around Pan's cable. The crotch of her silk, designer slacks ripped wide open.

Linda Ann Finn, Alice Nell Puffin and Principal Gunderson, who had followed Bo and Wanda Mensch to the winding metal stairs, were now joined by Noel and his grandmother on the platform that continued to sway from side to side.

"Who's on duty at the maitre d' stand?" Bo asked Noel, his head going from side to side as he tried to watch the approaching quintet of screaming, swearing women and estimate any lost revenue at the unattended entrance at the same time.

"Juan took over for us," said Noel, his arm wrapped around his grandmother's shoulders.

"My goodness," they all said at once, noticing five clawing, screaming, kicking women approach them at a high rate of speed, Noel's grandmother adding, "How marvelously exciting."

The crowd below believing they were being introduced to a new form of adult entertainment changed their shouts to repeating: "Puntang!"

Regis, Rommie and Reggie shifted into, *Hang on, Snoopy.*

Amanda and Arvia hung on for dear life to a mixture of cables, legs, vinyl boots and whatever else they could grab, their legs frantically kicking, unintentionally, with the cadence of the chanting below. The arcs of the five had picked up even more speed.

"Another sinner repents!" shouted Pastor Puffin. He was sweating so profusely that the pages to his Bible were soaked and sticking together in clumps. He has never felt so full of the Lord's grace since his ordination in Scotland and his honeymoon night with Alice Nell who had him hollering at the top of his voice, "I'll take the high road and yee keep taking that low road, Lassie!"

Bo tried to step over a sad, frightened and despondent Hans who decided to stand up and respectfully snap to attention. "Herr Bo," said Hans, the front of Bo's crotch in his face, one leg over each of Hans's shoulder. "I failed you."

Bo looked down at Hans and calmly said, "Please, Sylvester Mendenhall, put me down." He tried to wiggle off of Hans's shoulders. "Please put me down and help me get those girls to safety." Bo didn't care if his new found fame and fortune was disintegrating before his watery eyes. He knew that safeguarding human life was more important than money. But, not by much. Then the platform and spiral metal staircase let out a groan and every hand that could grab for something to grab latched onto railings and an assortment of human limbs for safety and support.

Ben looked at Sam and said, "This isn't good, is it, Mister Sam?" He took one hand off the railing and reached for the control panel that was dangling by its black umbilical cord waiting for a command. He reached too far, slipped and fell off the platform just as the five women were swinging back, all five an abject picture of total fear.

The crowd below loved the show; their chance of witnessing a celebrity marriage now included entertainment as well as versions of sky diving. Some changed their shouts to, "Fly! Fly! Fly" while others, mostly men, started shoving toward the men's room continuing with their shouts of, "Puntang!"

Ben felt that what was happening had been his fault. All he knew is he had to make up for the mess he caused. As his mother, Amanda Newton, Matilda, Peter and Pan neared the platform, he made a desperate lunge to somehow save them. His lunge resulted in his grabbing onto Pan's vinyl boots. Five aerialists now became six. "Oh, shit!" Ben yelled, joining the other screaming and panic stricken bodies and sailed out over the crowd.

"I heard that, Benoni," said Arvia, her face picture framed by a pair of black, vinyl boots. "You know we don't talk like that at Dogwood or anywhere else," she said.

"I'm sorry I failed you," said Hans, continuing to stand at rigid attention, begging forgiveness from Bo who was standing and looking like a person with no IQ.

"You didn't fail anyone," said Bo. "You were just doing your job." He paused. "Do you still have your balls?"

"I think so, Herr Bo."

"Good," said Bo. He turned and his eyes appeared to pop out of his head.

Hans had grabbed Bo from behind, lifted him up and placed him on the body guard's right shoulder. Then, doing a series of joyful pirouettes, shouted, "Dunka Schoen!" His pirouettes almost kicked Noel, his grandmother, the principal, Wanda Mensch, Linda Ann Finn, Alice Nell Puffin and Sam down the stairs of the platform.

As Hans complete his third pirouette, Bo saw six cages with the go-go girls appearing to be on a collision course with the six frantic, clawing, screaming people suspended and kicking from the ends of three cables. "Oh, shit," said Bo seeing the combination of swinging cages and suspended bodies ready to meet and greet each other in mid-air. "Put me down, you stupid Kraut!" he shouted.

Sam latched onto the railing with his right hand and leaned out off the platform. "We've got to get them in," he said to Bo, his body stretching out as far as he could make it stretch.

Bo tried to get off of Hans's shoulders, but his employee wouldn't let go of his grip. "Hans, put me down!" yelled out Bo.

Hans bent down, gave Bo a boost off his shoulder and politely sent him head first over the railing.

Without hesitation, Wanda Mensch latched onto the white belt of Bo's uniform pants, her tiny body crashing into the railing that started to give way. Hans grabbed onto Wanda. "Hang on, Fraulein. Hang on," he said, pulling Wanda into the middle of the platform as Bo rolled over the railing and landed on his back. The metal platform was now visibly swaying.

"Repent! Repent!" yelled Pastor Puffin into the microphone while Obadiah and Emerine stayed kneeling, their arms thrust up to Heaven.

Reggie, Rommie and Regis began to play, "Praise the Lord and Pass the Ammunition" a World War II song they remembered as kids.

Linda Ann Finn, hearing the song, began her impersonation of Barbra Streisand trying to force the lyrics to Hello Dolly into the World War II melody. Alice Nell Puffin and Lucia Gunderson, each taking an arm of Linda Ann Finn, started to cautiously take the first steps down the spiral stairs from the platform.

Bo could see a collision of cages, cables and humanity about to happen. "Sam, get the other rail!" he yelled out. "Hans, grab our pants by the waist and hang on for dear life. Here they come." Wanda latched onto Bo's white belt again as he reached for his sister. He ended up with her blouse in his hand. Sam reached for Amanda's outstretched hand. Just before their arc started them back out over the crowd, Sam, hanging onto the platform railing, saw and felt Amanda suspended in space. He braced himself and pulled; Hans set himself and also braced and pulled. Amanda's dead weight surprised them, but Sam hung on until he had her safely on the platform. The other five continued out in another faster, shorter arc, their feet skimming the tops of the cages.

"Get down from here and head for Bo's office," said Sam to Amanda. "It's just opposite the fire exit door."

"But, my baby," she protested. "I want my baby."

"You'll get your baby on the next pass. But, it's too crowed up here. This whole platform could come crashing to the floor." He gave her a kiss on the tip of her nose. "Now get." He draped her blouse around her shoulders and looked at Hans. "Take her down to Bo's office."

"But I only take orders from Herr Bo," said Hans, not moving.

The only part of Sam's body that moved was his eyes.

"I'm going, Herr Sam," he said, spitting out his words. "I'm going!"

Bo looked at Wanda. "You're off this platform too," he said. "Help take care of Tinker Bell's mother."

Sam and Bo each grabbed a railing and reached out again, Bo for Ben and Sam for Arvia as the mother and son pair saw the platform racing for them. "Oh, shit," they both cried out as mother and son felt their feet hit the platform perfectly and welcomed being yanked to safety. That was the only welcome they received. Orders to get off the platform and head to Bo's office were yelled at them and they followed those orders without a word.

The crowd below continued to shout and holler totally drowning out Linda Ann Finn's screeching solo that had been added with theatrics and waving arms that almost knocked Lucia Gunderson and Alice Nell Puffin down the spiral staircase. She reached the last step of the platform looking for applause. All she received was a backside view of Lucia Gunderson and Alice Nell Puffin just as they neared the fire exit door.

Sam and Bo saw Matilda and the two kindergarten teachers heading on a collision course toward them. Compounding the collision was the appearance of six cages with a go-go dancer in each. "Look out, Princess!" shouted Sam, just as the cages came up snaring the three wires supporting the trio turning them into a single twisted strand of cable.

CHAPTER 5

<u>Pastor Puffin, His Sinners and the Bunny Hop</u>

(Izzy and Achmed)

B etween Cap'n's Kids music, Pastor Puffin's preaching and Obadiah and Emerine's repenting, the chanting crowd now heard the shrieks coming from the six go-go cages. The cries of jungle animals in panic as King Kong rumbled after Fay Wray couldn't compare with what echoed from the dancers. The cables holding their cages seemed to enjoy being tangled and twisted into a macabre version of the *Stroll* and *Watusi.*

Had the dancers, Peter, Pan and Tinker Bell had the presence of mind to look down at their audience thye would have witnessed humanity lacking all signs of being human. There was a foggy layer of smoke hanging over the crowd. Most of smoke coming from cigars, pipes, joints, bongs and even several hookahs, but no cigarettes. La Tinkerbelle's a Go-Go enforced a strict ban on cigarette smoking since the unhealthy habit had been legislated out of existence. More liquor was worn that ingested and shuffling feet, jamming elbows, along with pushing and shoving and an occasional bite from Charles in the boutique, were the only evidence of disco dancing at La Tinkerbelle's.

Those who were lucky enough to get into the discotheque found themselves stacked in a sea of vertical humanity around the band stand. The other two choices were being crushed at the bar or engaged in the 1950's collegiate fad version of telephone booth cramming. Trying to get in or out of the boutique or the men's room were other bruise causing experiences. A wall of customers surged forward at the front door like a tidal wave, eyes barely able to shift in sockets to catch a glimpse of Captain Hookette, before flowing back in slow motion to the parking lot outside the front entrance where they had started.

Juan Ponce de Leone had been joined by Jesus at the maitre d' stand to collect the ten dollar cover charge. All traces of a Spanish accent were missing as they shouted out how much the waiting customers had to pay. The only traces of Spanish coming from them were the descriptive, derogatory words indicating a male or female tacked on to the end of, "ten dollars."

Peter, Pan and Tinker Bell lifted their feet and began tip-toeing across the top of the six cages. Matilda didn't shriek or scream. The fear of what her mother would do to her once she was back on the platform and safe took care of her dream of having a career in the performing arts. Peter and Pan didn't shriek or scream either. Kindergarten teachers don't raise their voices. But Peter and Pan weren't sitting at tiny tables in tiny chairs talking to five year olds under the watchful eyes of Moses. In coherent voices, several steps above conversational level and a wrung or two below ear drum busting, they explained to their employer, Bo Pepperwall who was watching them from the platform: "Get us down from here, you ass hole!"

The color drained from Matilda's face. Even her mask couldn't hide her shock. "My goodness," she thought, "I never knew kindergarten teachers used that kind of language. Peter Pan never did in anything I ever read about him."

As the trio's feet skipped off the last cage, they continued a slow, agonizine arc toward the platform, their rate of speed having been cut by the snared cables. They now resemblined a trio of geriatric Tarzan's swinging on tangled vines.

Bo and Sam braced again and reached out, two pairs of hands for three pairs. The platform was almost in reach. Hands grabbed, muscles stretched with accompanying groans, the spiral staircase adding its own version of groans, while fingers clawed air. Matilda was safe in her father's arms while four clenched fists sailed back out over the crowd and Bo hung by one hand from the railing his feet frantic for a surface to tap dance on. Peter and Pan were livid. "Bo Pepperwall," Peter yelled, one fist shaking, the other sprouting an extended middle finger. "You stupid bastard get us down from here."

Bo added his version of a groan along with a grunt as he kicked and pulled his way back to the platform. Sam, after being sure his daughter was safe, gave him a hand. "I'll get you down," shouted Bo back to them. "Heck, I belong to Mensa."

"Hang on to your brainy balls, Pepperwall," screamed Pan as the arc back to the platform now included two butts bouncing across the tops of the six cages. "I'm gonna turn them into peanut brittle when I get my hands on you."

Peter and Pan's arc was cut short by a jolt as their two cables tangled with Matilda's empty one and the last go-go cage. The girls hung like two marionettes just out of reach of Bo's and Sam's hands, their eyes even with the platform. "Pepperwall, you schmoe," shouted Pan, her fist shaking and middle finger still extended. "Get ready to have your peanuts brittled."

The six cages began clanging together like out of tune church bells but the crowd below barely heard the clangs, scrapes and screams. They could only see the bottoms of the cages. What they heard was Reggie, Rommie and Regis shift into their arrangement of, *Sing You Sinners*. The new song was being punctuated by Pastor Puffin's shouts of, "Hallelujah."

Pastor Puffin was elated as he watched Obadiah and Emerine Randall walk across the bandstand on their knees, hands spread out to the Heavens as tears streamed down their faces.

"Save us from our life of sin," Obadiah pleaded in his southern drawl. "Cleanse our souls."

"Hallelujah," shouted Pastor Puffin, his Bible waving back and forth spraying the first two rows of customer around the bandstand with his perspiration. The only thing that could have given him more pleasure was a chilled gin 'n tonic.

"Pronounce the holy bonds of matrimony upon your humble servants who have lived in sin for too long," pleaded Emerine, her hands clutching her tambourine in both a plea and a prayer.

"It's them," yelled out a hysterical female customer standing next to the bandstand, the effects of four Stingers for lunch on an empty stomach taking away most of her eye sight and deadening several lobes of her brain. "The Clerical Crier and the Monetary Movie Miz are getting married!" She started to faint, but there was nowhere for her to fall. "Oh my, married in front of me." She finished fainting and stood wedged in between a crowd that once again started surging toward the bandstand, carrying her vertical body with them.

For the first time in the history of go-go dancing, a dancer's hair moved. The go-go dancers didn't care. The frenzied shaking, rattling and rolling of their cages had turned their cookie cutter lacquered quaffs into six U.S. Post Office mug shots of crazed women strung out on some basement brewed designer drug.

The metal cages continued playing a deadly game of bumper pool and their version of, *Church Bells May Ring*. Grinding moans came from the hoists motor and the faint signs of smoke began to emit from the greasy black metal housing.

"Get us out of here!" yelled the go-go dancers, as the confused cables holding their cages continued to twist around each other forming a giant braid.

"We repent!" yelled Obadiah and Emerine still on their knees and looking up at Pastor Puffin, salty tears stinging their eyes, blurring their vision. Obadiah thought the Lord was making him go blind when he got his first glance at what was going on above him. He gouged at his eyes with his fists and his eye sight worsened.

Outside the boutique where Frank and Charles had earlier watched Tinker Bell, Peter and Pan, gushing like two proud parents attending their child's first dance recital, they now witnessed a catastrophe mushrooming around them. Their heads were locked looking up, Adam's apples lodged somewhere between their esophagus and sphincter muscle, and saw smoke from the overtaxed motor crawling across the ceiling. "Thank, God, she's safe," they said in unison as they made out a figure in a black mask being helped down the spiral stairs. Frank and Charles looked at one another, nodded and headed back inside the empty boutique.

"I'll get the Erte," said Frank.

"And, I'll get the money," said Charles calmly. "Presidents heads all in the same direction," he continued. "No folded corners or creases." He then gave Frank a thumb up signal.

"That's why we get paid what we get paid," added Frank, as he set the Erte outside the accordion door. "As soon as you get the receipts stashed in your pockets, I think we should see if we can offer assistance to our sisters." Then Frank said, "Put any change, what little there is, in your thong."

"No room, silly," said Charles.

After securing the gate, the two boutique managers, Charles with every part of his clothing showing bulges and Frank lugging the Erte, as if it were priceless, headed for the fire exit door area. Shoving wasn't necessary. There was no one to shove except several rollerblading pirates carrying trays. The crowd had swarmed around the band stand trying to get a glimpse of the historical wedding.

From their different vantage points, the go-go dancers, Peter, Pan, Sam and Bo saw the snarled cables and tangled cages. The go-go dancers had a hard time seeing anything through their hair and didn't care. The only thing that mattered was staying alive.

Three things mattered to Peter and Pan. Getting back safely to the platform and out of the crotch chaffing harnesses they wore were the first two things. Of paramount importance was throwing Bo off the same platform. Neutering him first had entered their minds.

The crowd still didn't know about the flames lashing out and gobbling up everything they could high up over their heads. They wouldn't have cared. They were part of a history making event. What was taking place before their eyes would be something they could share with their grandchildren or brag about to their envious friends. They might even be seen as part of the evening news, if they didn't get crushed to death or end up being part of what the flames were devouring.

Izzy Inman, who for some unknown urge, had gotten out of bed early and had his breakfast at noon instead of at four, sensed urgency. Accompanying his feeling of urgency was his nose showing traces of blood. Izzy nose bleeding was a sure sign that there was a story somewhere in Chicago that needed his creative touch. Izzy had no doubt that the somewhere was La Tinkerbelle's. That morning he had been out the front door of his condo located east of Chicago's landmark Water Tower in full stride. Achmed, his full-time taxi cab driver, had been surprised to see, Mr. Izzyman, as he called him, getting an early start.

"Achmed," Izzy had said with a smile. "Drop me off at that same disco joint you did the other night."

"Pronto, Tonto," replied Achmed, as he flipped the red flag on his meter that wasn't connected. Izzy Inman paid him more than he could earn driving a cab for real, but Achmed enjoyed playing with the red flag.

Izzy's bulbous nose sensed the kinds of stories that made tabloids rich and famous and kept average housewives from taking their own lives because of day-to-day boredom. As he rode in the cab, he had to hold a handkerchief to his bleeding nose. The smell of blood, even though it was his own, had him checking the inside pocket of his suit coat to see if he had his tiny spiral notebook and gold engraved fountain pen. His near hand grabbed for the door handle as the cab came to a dead stop in traffic that extended a half mile from La Tinkerbelle's. His nose had begun to bleed even more. "This is a day that will live in infamy," he said to Achmed, as he slipped him an extra ten spot. "Use the sidewalk."

"Pronto, Tonto," said Achmed, exposing a smile that showed off two rows of crooked, sparkling white teeth topped with gold.

Izzy patted himself on the back for his creative infamy line and made it a point to toast it with a customary glass of Chartreuse when he got to La Tinkerbelle's. After all, it would be free and Izzy Inman hadn't paid for a drink in Chicago in fifteen years. The red blots on Izzy's handkerchief grew bigger by the time the cab reached La Tinkerbelle's parking lot.

Achmed kept laying on the horn as if he were driving the cab through the streets of Cairo, his home. People scattered, cussed at him and some even pounded on the trunk as the cab kept going, several shouting, "Watch where you're going, camel jockey!"

"Pronto, Tonto," he kept repeating, until the cab's front end was touching the side of Juan's valet hut.

"Its gawl darn bedlam," said Izzy to Achmed.

"Pronto, Tonto," replied the calm cab driver.

Izzy Inman never swore, cursed or used any type of profanity. He did, however, enjoy sporadic interludes to his favorite adult bookstore. Before venturing into the underbelly of literature, Izzy put on a grey wig, black overcoat and derby hat that made him look like an obese character on "Laugh In" and would say to Achmed, "I'll be awhile."

Achmed knew that his command of English wasn't necessary when dropping his boss off a block from Mr. Izzyman's haunt, *Belles-Lettres.* That location Achmed understood. Translated it meant he had several hours that were his.

"I'll be awhile," said Izzy, standing in front of the jammed packed main entrance to the disco.

"Pronto, Tonto," said Achmed ever so politely. The moment Izzy started for the disco's entrance, Achmed engaged the meter mechanism and started looking for fares.

"Put it on my tab," Izzy said to Juan Ponce de Leone and Jesus who had taken over the maitre d' stand when Noel had left with his grandmother.

"Si," said Juan, recognizing Izzy from his picture in the Daily Examiner. "Let me escort you safely through this crowd," said Juan, giving a nod to Jesus to mind the store. He hoped his gesture might get him a mention in Izzy's column. "My name is Juan, Senor Inman," he said, the Spanish accent returning. "That's Juan Ponce de Leone." He looked over his shoulder at the wide-eyed columnist who was holding a bloody handkerchief to his nose. "That with four es," he quickly added.

Izzy couldn't believe the chaos. If he could have reached behind his back with his puffy, short arms, he would've patted himself to death. He looked at Juan. "Looks like the Miz and the Crier lost their hideaway," he said, with a smirk that radiated he was the instigator.

"Looks like you just made it in time for the wedding," replied Juan. "If you got here earlier, I doubt if even I, Juan Ponce de Leone, that's with four es, could have helped you."

Izzy let out a sarcastic laugh. "Ain't no crowd big enough. Ain't no mob unruly enough to keep old Izzy away from what he has created," he said, his nose twitching, the red blots on his handkerchief no longer growing. "Bert Lancaster was a rank amateur after what he did to Tony Curtis."

"This I did not know," said Juan. "Those guys were before my time."

"Izzy let out another sarcastic laugh. "Too bad," he said, his nose twitching as he examined his stained handkerchief. "Do I smell something burning?"

Smoke billowed in thicker clouds from the motor in batches of black and grey accompanied by the acrid smell of burning electrical wires. Droplets of hissing sparks floated down missing the crowd but not the backstage and storage areas. In spite of having its heart and soul turned to molten wire, the hoist chugged along its mono-rail support, its gears coughing a melody of raspy, grinding notes. Then with a final gasp and a belch of flame the hoist came to rest at the end of the platform. There was a last whirl of gears and the six cages holding the frantic and hysterical go-go girls started straight down in a normal decent to the staging area below as if nothing had happened.

Peter and Pan dangling like frightened marionettes from their cables and harnesses stretched for the extended hands of Sam and Bo. In a rapid fire sequence of counting out one, two, three, Bo used muscles he never knew he had as he and Sam pulled Peter and Pan to safety. Below, the cages touched down on the concrete floor like six fluffy feathers landing on a grassy field. Six wire doors sprung open below and the go-go dancers, looking as if they had stood facing a tropical hurricane, stumbled out. They were tripping over John Brown's unconscious body still propped next to the fire exit door blocking their path. Six pairs of hands almost shredded the lawyer's suit from his body as he was unceremoniously yanked aside.

Carefree sparks and hungry flames fueled by decades of grease and dirt continued to shoot out of the deceased motor lighting up the club's black ceiling like the pyrotechnic display Bo had dreamed of providing for his customers. The energized flames licked their way across the ceiling enjoying their feasting on the buffet of grease, oil and hanging back drops.

Bo had Peter and Pan safely in front of him, all of them clutching the hand railings and taking the stairs as fast as the spiked heels on their simulated patent leather boots could navigate the grating. Threats of neutering Bo Pepperwal had been put on hold. Sam was right behind, the last off the platform. The platform was now swaying so badly he felt himself being bounced off the railings on each side.

"Hang on," Bo shouted to Peter and Pan. "Keep going no matter what." They were near the bottom and Bo murmured, "If there is a real Peter Pan, please get these kids safely down."

He looked up, almost missed a step and tripped. He grabbed the railing with his right hand his momentum spinning and turning him so that he was looking up. What he saw gave him a shiver. A waterfall of sparks cascaded down from the high ceiling. "Peter Pan, I apologize, but I'm turning this over to God," he said, his breathing in gasps. "And I promise to tell Noel everything about seeing my brother-in-law getting killed."

The go-go girls coughed and panted for breath and looked bewildered standing in the parking lot in sunshine and fresh air. In minutes they were escorted to Juan's Valet Parking shack by two of the attendants who smiled at the sight of two mini-skirts dangling from the crash bar of the fire exit door.

Flames continued to explode from the motor, orange tongues licking at the edges of a cheap black theatrical curtain trimmed in gold braid that hung down covering the back wall of La Tinkerbelle's. The curtain was another of Bo's bargains purchases from John's Junk Store. "This baby's a real treasure," John Cinderella had said to Bo, showing him a corner of the thick velvet curtain with gold tassels he had taken from the alley behind where the Will Rogers stood before the northwest side neighborhood movie theatre became a pile of rubble.

The crowd was engrossed in watching Pastor Rufus Puffin about to pronounce Obadiah and Emerine husband and wife and had no idea there was a fire spreading in all directions high above them. Neither did the pastor who bordered on feeling beatified knowing he had brought two redeemed souls back to his flock. What he desperately needed more than ever, even before launching a new crusade to convert the pagan crowd into soldiers of Christ in the Den of Inequity, was a gin 'n tonic; this one a double.

As Sam cleared the final metal step, the swaying spiral staircase took its last sway, teetering and crashing against the factory's brick wall before coming to rest at a forty five degree tilt. He momentarily put his arms around the shoulders of the badly shaken Peter and Pan and asked and asked, "Are you okay?" Before they could ansnwer, his hands gave them each a gentle push toward the door. "Ladies, forget about neutering your boss," he said not joking. "Get out of here now!" He watched the two kindergarten teacher's step around John Brown and squeeze through the opening of the fire escape door.

Bo's eyes were fixed on the ceiling. "This isn't good, Sam," he said, watching the flames grab at anything that would satisfy their insatiable appetite.

"Now there's a profound statement, Boss," said Sam, as he watched chunks of flaming curtain float down landing on the cubicles of stacked wooden pallets that made up Bo's office and the girls' dressing room.

The pile of newspapers Bo had slept on the night before his life took the world's fastest trip from flop to fame and then to flame were history. "We've got to clear this place out, Sam," he said, watching more chunks of flaming curtain flutter down just as his desk burst into flames. His eyes were calculating, plotting and looking like he was putting together the pieces to another Mensa puzzle. "We've got to stay calm. We've got to be cool. What we don't need is a panic." He felt himself wanting to scream out, FIRE! He didn't and then said to Sam, stammering, "I already told the Almighty that I'm going to Noel when we get out of here." He glanced at the fire exit door and saw Charles, his pockets and trousers bulging with money that made him look like the Pillsbury Doughboy. Frank embraced the Erte using his body to protect it from any errant collision with a patron. At times, he looked as if he were dancing the *Lambeth Walk*. "Get out to Juan's shack and see if you can help out," said Bo, his statement sounding like a suggestion because he knew Charles was not one to take orders without going into at least a minimum of a fifteen minute snit. He knew they didn't have fifteen seconds. Then he saw John Brown.

The lawyer, still out cold, savored his dream world of six go-go dancers having their way with him, living their sexual fantasies to the fullest while praising his sexual prowess and lauding his performance in graphic erotic terms that would have put Henry Miller to shame. No other females ever lauded John Brown for his performance in bed. Cheerleaders and a few female fans shouted what cheerleaders and female fans shouted at football games. Their exuberant shouts of, "rah-rah," were not connected to a dorm room, the back seat of a car or on a blanket spread out on a farmer's field in the Urbana, Illinois moonlight. John Brown's dream had him being carried from the farmer's field on the shoulders of the six go-go dancers. Even the spirit of Quintin Bell was impressed with his former football teammate's dream. John Brown's nose twitched and he coughed.

The heavy piercing smoke had no place to go but to crawl down the walls of the disco. The fire exit door had been propped open by two of Juan's parking attendants, Jorge and Vincente, who had escorted the go-go dancers to the parking hut minutes ago. A stiff Chicago fall breeze tried to get in but collided head on with the heavy smoke trying to get out. Bo could see people still trying to gain admittance through the front entrance. Noel and his grandmother who had left the platform returned to the maitre d' stand at her request to relieve Juan. "Oh, please, Noel," she had said sweetly. "I need to feel like a captain steering my own ship again,"

Noel gave his grandmother her way knowing it would only be for a few seconds. Those few seconds saw his grandmother collect another one hundred and thiry dollars before the fire engulfed the entire ceiling and was now racing down the walls. She was moving her two index fingers together after stuffing the final ten down the front of her blouse. Mildred stood alongside Noel, her two index fingers pointing at unruly customers who were pushing and shoving. "Naughty, naughty," she said, as she slowly rubbed one index finger over the other, her head going slowly from side to side. Her last words as the temporary captain were, "Thank you," as she snatched a final ten dollar out of an extended hand. Then she felt her grandson's hand on her arm pulling her toward the front door.

Peter and Pan, along with Charles and Frank, had joined Matilda and the six go-go dancers at Juan's shack in the back parking lot. Matilda was met by two very confused and agitated mothers.

Hans was standing just inside the fire exit door shouting at Bo: "Herr Bo! Herr Bo! *Beeil dich!*"

Bo looked toward the bandstand where the Cap'n's Kids had

started playing, "Just a Closer Walk with Thee" a traditional song, Pastor Puffin believed, that honored the bride and groom. Regis, Reggie and Rommie tried to correct the sweating, red-faced minister, but he wasn't listening. Pastor Puffin, the newlyweds, Obadiah and Emerine and Cap'n's Kids couldn't believe what they began hearing. Sporadic clapping started coming from the crowd. In moments, a loud, rhythmic beat began to drown out the strains to, "Just a Closer Walk with Thee." Before he could fathom what was going on around him, Pastor Puff thought he heard the low bass chanting of, "Sinners, sinners, sinners!" Low didn't stay low for long. Obadiah and Emerine were mortified. Pastor Puffin was elated. He almost swallowed the microphone shouting, "Yes, you are!" after each crowd chant of, "sinners." Pastor Puffin looked to the heavens and saw sparks. Dense smoke subdued the bright oranges, reds and yellows clawing across the ceiling. He saw chunks of flaming debris falling to the floor behind Bo's office, the girls' dressing room, Ramon's salon and the kitchen area. Pastor Puffin knew this was an omen from God. "He sees all," he screamed into the microphone as loud as one of Obadiah's better hog calls. "He knows all!" One of the speakers crackled, popped and hissed and went dead. The flames of God's displeasure had Pastor Puffin craving his gin 'n tonic more than ever, this drink served directly from the bottle. He glanced toward the bar to see if he could get someone to roller skate over his libation. He needed it to help him save more souls and to quell the Almighty's anger. The bar was empty. Then he saw why. One end was on fire.

Hans rushed up to Bo, clicked his heels and gave him his best Hiel, Hitler salute. "Herr, Bo," he stated excitedly. "Herr,

Bo. For your safety, the safety of your customers and the good of the Fatherland you must get out now."

Bo stood like General Pepperwall's statue minus the horse, slashing rapier and the bird droppings. The only part of him that moved was his mind as it formulated a plan to evacuate La Tinkerbelle's.

"Oust with you," said a frustrated Hans. He dropped into a squat, picked Bo up like a sack of rye and plopped him over his shoulder, ready to carry his boss out the door to safety.

Bo blinked. "Put me down, you Nazi numbskull," he screamed.

Hans was stunned. "But, Herr Bo, I wasn't even born then. How could I be a Nazi?" He squatted back down and gently rolled Bo off his shoulder. "Please, Herr Bo," he said respect-fully. "You must leave now."

"Sam, you and Hans follow me," said Bo, the gears to his plan meshing without a grind.

Just then John Brown had gotten to his hands and knees and was trying to regain some resemblance of balance. He thought he was hallucinating when he saw who appeared to be Bo, Sam and Hans run into a cloud of black smoke. "Holy shit," he muttered, as he stood and teetered from side to side. The billowing smoke drifted toward him, reaching out for his mouth and nose, burning his eyes. This was no mirage; no psychedelic image fostered by Timothy Leary. He knew exactly what he had to do and he did it; staggering out the fire exit door gasping, he muttered, "Save your ass, Scats." Then he tripped and stumbled his way through the maze of parked cars as if he were once again a star running back carrying the football. Several stiff arms to the front hoods of four parked cars and he was at the valet parking hut. He could see Matilda, Peter, Pan, the go-go dancers, Amanda Newton and Arvia all huddled together.

When he got to the hut he coughed, gagged and reached for Arvia's hand. "Thank God your safe," he said, still feeling dazed and wondering why his crotch hurt. "I'm getting you out of this nut house right now." He pulled at her hand.

John Brown began to wonder why his crotch hurt even more. He began to wonder why his dizziness returned like a flash of lightning. There was no time for him to question why he was on his way down to the floor of Juan's hut even though, under normal conditions, he wouldn't have set foot in the hut. There were things in John Brown's world that were believable, explainable, like the letter of the law. What wasn't believable, although explainable and understood by everyone in the hut except John Brown, was the reason why Arvia Pepperwall Bell, reluctant socialite, night club owner and mayor of Glen Forest on the Watercourse had jammed her right knee into his balls.

As Bo, Sam and Hans cut their way through the smoke to get to the bandstand, they saw Frank and Charles standing at the entrance to the boutique. "I thought I told you guys to help out at Juan's hut," he said, as he and the other two watched Frank wrestling with unlocking the accordion security door.

"You did and we did," said Charles interrupting an animated conversation he was having with three women. "We thought we'd come back here and see if there was any money we forgot." Then showing his frustration he turned his attention back to the three women but kept talking to Bo. "I was trying to explain to these three members of the feminine gender that the boutique was closed for the day and we'd be having a fire sale tomorrow."

Bo blinked and realized that the three potential customers were the new principal of the Glen Forest on the Watercourse High School, the Glen Forest Chief of Police's wife and his late brother-in-law's secretary, Wanda Mensch. Bo's black, weary blood shoot eyes made contact with Wanda's bland green orbs and he felt the same spark that had hit him earlier in the day. "Please, lovely lady,"he said to Wanda, "take you and your friends and go out that door there." He calmly pointing at the fire exit door. "I'll meet you at the parking valet hut."

"Is that a promise?" asked Wanda, the soot coating her face unable to hide the innamored look.

Bo nodded and watched the three walk hurriedly toward the fire exit and disappear into the smoke.   Then he heard, "Achtung!"

Hans, seeing the crowd around the bandstand, looked at Sam and then to Bo and said: "Herr, Bo, you and your employee must follow me. I'm giving you both a direct order."   Then with Bo and Sam behind him, he shouted, "Achtung!" and charged into the crowd like a human wrecking ball out of control. Patrons scattered like helpless milk bottles in a carnival arcade baseball toss as Hans barreled head down toward the bandstand.

Obadiah, confused about the chants of, "Sinners" realized that he was now married to someone old enough to be his grandmother and he was repenting for sins he didn't know he committed. His confusion was added to by Alice Nell Puffin who had veered away from Lucia Gunderson and Linda Ann Finn to return to the bandstand and be at her husband's side. She now had a desire to convert sinners. Alice Nell snuck up behind Obadiah, wrapped her arms around him, gave him a hug and whispered in his ear, "Praise the Lord." Then she stuck her tongue in his ear.

Obadiah moved his head up with a jerk yanking Alice Nell's tongue from his ear with a pop. The motion sent her head back and had her looking up at the ceiling. "Have mercy on me, a sinner," she muttered, knowing the flames and destruction were meant for her. She watched as Obadiah picked up Emerine from her kneeling position in front of Pastor Puffin and said, "Come on, Emerine, we've got us some souls to save." He looked at a sweating Pastor Puffin and said, "Excuse me, Revered, but I'm going to need this." He ripped the microphone from Pastor Puffin's sweaty hand just as Alice Nell latched onto her husband's other arm. "Say, Amen," she said to her husband, her eyes focused on the ceiling. "And pray for me."

Obadiah latched on to Emerine's hand and began dragging her with a series of several clumsy dance step strides toward Rommie, Reggie and Regis. His hand covered the microphone while he kept glancing up at the ceiling watching the flames enjoy their gluttonous race. The trio of musicians glanced up. Without missing a beat they start playing, "I Don't Want to Set the World on Fire."

"No, gawl dang it," snapped Obadiah. "Bunny Hop, guys," he said, his hand still over the microphone. "Play the Bunny Hop!"

The three octogenarian band members gave a nod and, with Reggie counting out a, "Hop, hop, hop," and Regis stomping his boombass and shouting, "Hop-hop-hop!" the group swung into the Bunny Hop.

Obadiah removed his hand from the microphone; his hand

scrapping across the wire mesh normally would cause ear drums to revolt. Not this time. His best hog calling effort couldn't get the crowd's attention. He put his hands around Emerine's ample hips and nodded at Alice Nell to get her husband to join in behind him. He took three hopping steps to the edge of the bandstand, each hop met by a smash to the floor of Regis's boombass. As the trio continued playing the Bunny Hop, Obadiah jumped off the bandstand, spun around and lifted Emerine off by placing his hands on her waist. "Hop," he yelled to her as he set her down on the dance floor. In an instant he had Alice Nell Puffin by her hourglass figure and had set her down on the dance floor. "Hop," he yelled at her.

"How 'bout ya'll hop me instead," she said, just as her husband, Bible still in hand, landed beside her.

"Hop, Pastor, hop," ordered Obadiah as he waved to Regis, Rommie and Reggie to join the Bunny Hop line.

"Are you outta your mind?" Reggie asked Obadiah.

Obadiah looked up at the ceiling for his answer.

"Like, hop, cats," shouted Reggie to his two companions in the band. "Make like Peter Cottontail hopping along the bunny trail before our tails get burned off."

Obadiah, the microphone cable having reached its length, gave a tug on the cable and toppled over one of the amplifiers. Appearing as if the microphone had stuck in his throat, he let out a hog call of championship caliber: "Sueey, pig! Sueey, sueey, sueey, ya pig!" He took another quick glance up at the ceiling and shouted into the microphone, "Hey, ya'll, me and the Miz wants ya'll to join us in our special Arkansas wedding dance!"

"My God, it is her," muttered another crowd member.

Necks craned, heads turned and bodies jostled for a better position to view Izzy Inman's exposed celebrities. As Regis accentuated three more hops, Pastor Puffin yelled out, Sinners!" each time he hopped.

"If that's the Miz?" asked another patron. "She's got kind of a big ass if you ask me."

"Big is better than boney," said another.

"Bunny Hop!" hollered Obadiah into the microphone again. He saw Emerine turn around and he pointed at the front entrance. Alice Nell Puffin led her sweating, panting husband and they quickly grabbed several patrons to join them.

The crowd, excited about having a chance to a part of the wedding celebration, joined the Bunny Hop line making its way toward the front door just. Obadiah got through one third of a hop and a fourth of a hog call when the microphone jack plug was yanked from the amplifier. Most of the crowd clamored to grab a hold of Emerine's hips causing a huge distortion in the Bunny Hop's line. By the time they had hopped a dozen times, the back side of Emerine's white, sequined cocktail dress was minus any signs of even a single sequin and sporting five or six dozen smears resembling hand prints.

Emerine kept her smile, swatted at grabbing hands with her tambourine and kept knifing through the crowd to the door. Those in the crowd who tried to touch one of the newlyweds, cop a feel, grab a souvenir of clothing or some bodily part were met by Hans. Or, Hans met them in a head on charge.

"You vill hoppity-hippity like der leader of da band says," he commanded. "And, if you know what's good for you, you will be orderly!" He began shoving patrons toward the door. "Hoppity-hippity," he continued, his German for goose step, kicking patrons out of his way as he pushed harder, his knowing eyes taking quick glances up and calculating that he didn't have a second to spare.

Obadiah, Emerine and the Bunny Hop line behind them approached Noel. He stood stunned alongside his grandmother at the jammed front entrance as he looked at Obadiah, his eyes questioning. Obadiah answered his question by slowly looking up at the ceiling. One look on Noel's part had him reacting. The fire was now out of control.

Noel pulled out his Chicago Police shield and thrust it into the faces of those clogging the entranceway. "Police business!" he shouted. "The City of Chicago says we need an inter-mission!" he yelled. "First customers out the door get double their money back and free readmission!" He began shoving at the customers with both hands.."Help me make an opening to the street and I'll triple your money back."

"Oh, my," Noel's grandmother remarked. "Does this mean I'm getting fifteen for my orignial five?" Then she felt her arm almost being yanked out of its socket as Noel began dragging her out the door. "But, Noel," she protested. "They're doing that cute Bunny Hop."

"Hop this, Grandma," said Noel continuing to pull his grandmother to safety. Then he heard the German accent of Hans.

"Hippity-hoppity, fraulien," said Hans who had joined Noel to open up an escape route for the patrons who still hadn't realized the building they were in was on fire.

Bo pushed and shoved his way to Noel. "We've got to get these people out of here!" he shouted.

Noel gave him a clam look. "Got it under control, Boss," he

said. "No need to panic."

Out in the parking lot at the valet's hut, John Brown looked up at a sea of angry female faces. His crotch ached and so did his head. He looked at Arvia with contempt and said, "I'm going to sue your ass."

Arvia didn't say a word.

"Did you hear what I just said," he barked at Arvia. He was on his feet now standing inches from her face. "Is Her Honor the Mayor suffering from being hard of hearing along with being a frigid bitch?"

Arvia said nothing.

"And don't get any ideas about sneaking that knee into my balls again, you bitch," he warned. A grin came across his face. "I'm ready for any of your nonsense." Then John Brown's world went black again.

"But you weren't ready for my knee," said Amanda Newton, wiping her hands as if she had just dusted all of the book shelves in the library. "You weren't ready for me just the way I wasn't ready for you and the mayor the night you two perverts abused me at the country club."

"Well, done, Miss Newton," said Arvia as they both high fived. Arvia smiled at Amanda and Amanda smiled at Arvia. Then they heard the sound of sirens, lots of sirens.

In front, Noel and his grandmother had the front doors to the club propped open. Hans continued to force the crowd to the sides with his head being used as a battering ram. Laughing carefree patrons, most in various stages of intoxication, hopped out into the parking lot still unaware of the blaze inside the building even though black smoke was beginning to make its way out the open front entrace. The next thing Noel knew he was staring at Naomi Schmitt and her phallic symbol hand.

"Could you use this to keep the door propped open?" she asked, handing him the hand.

"I can," said Noel taking the hand and quickly shoving under the front door jamming it against the wall. It worked perfectly. He turned to Naomi and said, "Thanks."

Had their eyes not met they would have seen Izzy Inman enter the building. He had wormed his way into the club against the flow of humanity heading out the door. He had no idea why everyone was going in the opposite direction he was. Izzy was accustomed to attracting people not driving them away. Didn't they know he was the most powerful newspaper columnist in, perhaps, the Nation? Surely they had read his column. Didn't they know that when he sat down at a bar, any bar in Chicago, he was treated like royalty, his drinks free? Now, as he sat down at the bar, it was empty except for a layer of what he thought looked like smog. "Maybe I should write a column about air pollution in Chicago," he muttered, as he took a glance around the discotheque. There was no one there to treat him like royalty. Suddenly, one of the bartenders roller-skated up to him, set down an entire bottle of Chartreuse on the bar, the seal unbroken and said, "Great column. This is on the house." Then he skated after the tail end of the Bunny Hop line.

Izzy saw an empty glass on the bar, poured in a substantial amount of Chartreuse and lifted the glass in a toast. "After tonight, you elusive little angel," he said, referring to the one thing in life he wanted even more than his perceived power, "You're guaranteed mine." He gave a toast to the Pulitzer Prize for Journalism. He drained the glass and poured another drink. Then he looked down to the end of the bar to see if there was anyone there to share his toast. He put a strangle hold on the bottle of Chartreuse and screamed: "Fire!"

Standing alongside the open front entrance were Obadiah and Emerine, both directing traffic. Emerine yelled out, "Hop faster, ya'll, faster. The revenuers are a comin'."

Once outside in the parking lot, the crowd realized what was happening inside. Laughing was replaced by running but, as Bo had planned and hoped, there was no panic, just a continuous orderly move toward and across the busy street filling up the sidewalk in front of the housing project.

The housing project residents had lined the wire grated balconies to watch a swarm of hopping people spill out into La Tinkerbelle's parking lot and quickly filling it up and the street in front of the club. Sirens got louder as fire engines, ambulances, EMT vehicles, police cars and Paddy Wagons bounded into the lot, people scattering to avoid being run over. The mob of people found themselves weaving in and out of a giant spaghetti bowl of firefighting equipment and hoses being pulled into position.

The undercover cops did a quick sweep of the club. Their roller skates hummed along the concrete floor showing no respect for Bo's artistic skull and cross bones insignia which now looked like it was suffering from a case of scurvy. They were preceded by Izzy Inman, his Chartreuse bottle firmly in hand, waddling, coughing, his eyes burning. "Pulitzer Prize," he kept muttering in between coughing spasms. His nose had started bleeding again.

The horns and sirens continued blasting. In moments, the street outside had been shut down, all traffic re-routed and fire hoses snaked their way from a series of hydrants to the discotheque. Thick smoke poured out of the doors and from the club's faux leaded glass windows that had melted from the heat.

Bo was trying to believe what he was seeing. "Is everybody out?" he asked Sam. "Is my dedicated gang safe?"

Before Sam could answer, they saw Hans goose stepping and gagging his way out the front door, Heckle under one arm and Jeckle under the other, both cats covered in glitter. Hans walked up to Sam and Bo. He handed the cats to Sam and said to Bo, "All quiet on the western front, Herr Bo!" He coughed and a circle shaped cloud of black smoke looking like an old cigarette ad in New York's Time Square belched out.

"Are you sure everybody's out?" asked Bo again, his eyes fixed on the front entrance that was now blanketed with smoke as the fire fighters, breathing apparatus masks covering their faces, dashed into the building.

"Looks like it," said Sam cautiously. "I think so. I'm not...."

Rommie, Reggie and Regis stumbled through the front entrance still playing the Bunny Hop, each hop still punctuated with Regis's boombass and their gagging coughs. They were led by paramedics to one of the ambulances.

"Damn," muttered Bo. He gave a panicked glance at Sam. "We forgot the money!" His head rotated back and forth between the front entrance, Sam, the crowded parking lot and the fire engines. "The money, Sam, did you bring the money?" Before Sam could answer, Bo started back into the building. He got only one step before Sam put a horse collar on him.

Sam loosened his grip and put his arm around Bo's sagging shoulders. "Don't worry, Boss, Noel and his grandmother have some of it and Frank and Charles have the boutique's receipts. Juan has the parking money. The insurance will cover everything and you'll be back in business in no time."

Bo stopped, looked into Sam's eyes and asked, "Insurance?"

The two turned and walked in silence back toward Juan's hut. Just then Noel, dragging his grandmother by the hand, appeared. "The gangs all out of there," he said to Sam and Bo. "That newspaper guy was the last one out." His eyes and his grandmother's were the only part of their faces visible through a coating of heavy soot. "I saved what I could of the cover charges," Noel said to Bo, his index finger pointing at the front of his white shirt. "I never knew I had so many muscles."

Bo gave a resigned exhale and tried to smile. "Thanks, Noel."

"All of your people out?" asked Officer Pecker Peccarino, who hadn't been seen since he first organized the police officers to become owner-employees of La Tinkerbelle's. He appeared out of nowhere, concern written all over him.

Izzy Inman stood near Sam, Bo and the others, his bottle of Chartreuse still held in a strangle hold by his right hand. He stopped and waved at the scattered patrons, their eyes glued to the fire. Then he casually bent over and threw up all over himself.

"Thanks again, Noel," Bo said. "Remember what I was talking to you about earlier?"

"Kind of," said Noel.

"More than kind of," said Bo.   "I know who killed my brother-in-law."

"Kill," repeated Izzy Inman, his left coat sleeve wiping his mouth.   "Kill as in murder, as in Pulitzer Prize?"   His bottle of Chartreuse almost went half way down his throat.

CHAPTER 6

Officer Noel Jones and Judge Ransom Jones

(Cronkite's Cigar Club)

The only historical event to top the chaos taking place in La Tinkerbelle's parking lot was the scene of Atlanta burning in *Gone with the Wind*. The owners and employees of the disco were surrounded by enough fire equipment and personnel to control the devastation once caused by the O'Leary cow. They stood and stared huddled together in and around Juan Ponce de Leone's valet parking hut their sad frightened eyes peering out from soot covered faces, not believing. Then none could believe what they heard next.

"You're all under arrest," stated Noel Jones, his police shield displayed on the outside of his soiled white shirt tied at the navel, the cover charge money trying to spill out from the stuffed bulges at his chest and in the arms of his shirt sleeves. Noel kept poking stray bills back into his shirt with one hand and wiping what appeared to be tears away with the other while saying, "You have the right to remain...."

"Arrest," repeated Sam, a stunned look knocking half the soot from his face so he resembled a character from an old time minstrel show.

"Noel," said Bo, looking dumbfounded at the police officer

who minutes ago was his assistant maitre d' collecting a cover charge from the same patrons now spread out across the street and onto the sidewalks. "We're under arrest?" Bo asked. "I don't understand."

"Sorry, Bo," said Noel, glancing to the side street next to one end of the parking lot where a series of Paddy Wagons had lined up, their back doors open like whales ready to swallow a multitude of Jonah's and Geppedo's. He looked at the unconscious figure of John Brown, his thumb still stuck in his mouth and laying in a fetal position just to the side of Juan's hut. Then he looked at Arvia. "Sorry, Your Honor," he said to Arvia who was stunned like the others. "But, your friend," he stopped and pointed at John Brown on the pavement. "Well, your so-called friend filed criminal charges against all of you."

"Criminal charges," repeated Arvia, aghast. "Are you serious?"

"I wish I weren't," answered a sheepish Noel Jones. "That man there," he continued, nodding at John Brown. "He's accused all of you, including you, Your Honor, of a host of serious criminal charges."

"Even me," asked Mildred Farnsworth Pepperwall Jones. "Your grandmother?"

Noel nodded sheepishly. "That attorney there," he said nodding at John Brown again, "came up to me and shoved some legal papers in my face. He laughingly told me that La Tinkerbelle's was broke and going out of business and that a boat load of people were going to jail." Noel paused and gave a sad look at everyone including his fellow employees and officers. "He named all of you." He held up the papers for them to see.

"My heavens," said Arvia, reaching for the papers. "Did he write a Michener saga?"

"Sorry, Your Honor," Noel said, taking the papers back before Arvia could finish reading the charges John Brown had listed.

"I'm not surprised," said Sam, holding Heckle in one hand and Jeckle in the other. "But, what have we done that warrants our being arrested?"

Noel glanced down and spoke softly. "Among that man's complaints," he said, nodding at John Brown and unable to look at his co-workers and fellow officers who had worked security and were still dressed as pirates. "There's doing business without various city, county and state licenses."

All eyes turned to Bo.

CLICK/SNAP!

"That's why we're being arrested?" asked Arvia.

"Mr. Brown also filed a complaint with the EPA about the blatant disposing of hazardous materials in the Chicago River."

CLICK/SNAP!

"And that's why we're all being arrested?" asked Arvia again, her eyes fixed on her brother.

Noel cleared his throat, his sheepish look accompanied by a coating of genuine sorrow. "Well, Madam Mayor, there's more. Much more," he continued.

Arvia's face, as well as the faces of others, told him to continue.

"There's a possible violation of the Mann Act, ignoring Child Labor laws, serving alcohol to underage patrons, presenting pornographic movies and selling lewd adult oriented products."

CLICK/SNAP!

"Pornography," repeated Pastor Rufus Puffin, the Bartender's bible being held toward the heavens. "May the Lord have mercy on your souls?"

"Lewd adult oriented products," repeated Lucinda Gunderson in a whispered lisp to Linda Ann Finn and Alice Nell Puffin. "Do you think the boutique might have a fire sale after all of this jail nonsense gets settled?"

Alice Nell and Linda Ann gave a look that indicated that they liked Lucia's idea. "You will have a fire sale, won't you?" Linda Ann asked Bo.

CLICK/SNAP!

Noel took a deep breath. "There are also charges of indecent exposure, pandering, soliciting for prostitution and white slavery."

"I knew it," sputtered Amanda Newton, as she tried to get at Bo who was still standing dumb founded his right hand in the pocket of his white trousers that looked like he had crawled out of the burning building on his hands and knees.

Sam dropped Heckle and Jeckle who immediately gathered at Matilda's feet. He took Amanda by the arm. "Easy, Mandy," he said calmly. He nodded at John Brown still doubled up on the pavement. "Are you forgetting who filed these charges?"

"I'm ruined," a cry from behind Juan's hut rang out.

All heads turned to see a distraught Ramon, the owner of the exclusive beauty salon in La Tinkerbelle's. His right forearm was across his forehead, his left hand on the belt buckle of Charles who flanked him on the left. Frank was on his right. "Oh, fame, you fickle, fleeting bitch, how could you do this to me?" he asked, in a near shriek. "Why to me, hair stylist of the stars and the rich and famous?" He gave a glance towards Arvia. "And, you beautiful lady, my biggest challenge and success." Then he fainted into the combined arms of Charles and Frank.

Frank glanced at Charles and said, "He's a bigger homo than you are."

CLICK/SNAP!

"Are you sure about this, Noel?" asked Sam, still clutching Amanda's arm to keep her from possibly annihilating Bo and adding another criminal charge to the extensive list.

Noel nodded then his head barely turned in the direction to where the Paddy Wagons were waiting.

CLICK/SNAP!

Bouncing around in the back of one Paddy Wagon were Bo, Ben, Matilda, Arvia, Sam, Amanda Newton, Peter, Pan, Naomi Schmitt and Heckle and Jeckle. Officer Pecker Peccarino was the driver. In front with him was Officer Noel Jones, sandwiched between them both was an ecstatic and handcuffed Mildred Farnsworth Pepperwall Jones.

"Noel, I've never been arrested before," she said, her eyes aglow. She looked at Officer Peccarino. "Thank you for putting these on me," she said, displaying her handcuffed wrists to him.

"You're welcome, Mam," said Officer Peccarino.

"Young man," said Noel's grandmother politely. "Do you think I could turn on your siren?"

Officer Peccarino pointed and Noel's grandmother activated the siren. She clapped her handcuffed hands as best she could, let out a squeal of joy and savored her trip to jail.

In the second wagon were Obadiah, Emerine Randall, Regis, Rommie and Reggie, Hans, Frank, Charles, a prostrate and ashen looking Ramon and Sam's bartenders, all undercover cops, wondering why they had been busted. The third Paddy Wagon contained Lucia Gunderson, Rodney Bird Dog Pointer, Linda Ann Finn and her husband, Mickey. Rodney and Mickey had driven from Glen Forest on the Watercourse to get a first-hand view of the discotheque they had read about in Izzy Inman's column. They were walking toward Juan's parking hut when they were arrested. Chief Finn kept telling the Chicago Police officers that he was the Chief of Police of Glen Forest on the Watercourse. The Chicago cops ignored him, put both he and Rodney in handcuffs and ushered them both to the third Paddy Wagon where they saw a shaken Alice Nell Puffin clinging to the arm of her husband. Alice Nell was scared. The charges of prostitution had no sooner cleared the lips of Noel Jones when she thought her past had caught up to her. She had been arrested in Alabama for working the Naval Air Station along the Pensacola Panhandle. That was when, at an early desperate age, she jumped bail and fled the starry skies of Alabama for a life as Mrs. Rufus Puffin. She would sin no more. At least she thought sinning was in her past. Then she found herself in the small, prestige town of Glen Forest on the Watercourse, a pastor's wife, and meeting the consummate sinners, Quintin Bell and John Brown.

Also in the third Paddy Wagon were the waitresses still wearing their roller blades and roller skates wondering why they had been busted. On the floor of the third Paddy Wagon, his body, including his head being used as a foot rest by the others, was the still out cold John Brown sucking on his thumb.

Riding in the passenger seat of the third Paddy Wagon was Izzy Inman. He had conned the driver to let him ride up front with a promise he would get mentioned in his column that would be out the next day. Izzy couldn't believe his stroke of good luck. Now he had a follow up story to the wedding and the fire with one of the Preacher and the Miz heading to whatever Illinois State Penitentiary he thought would make for a good story and contribute to his being awarded a Pulitzer Prize. Life couldn't be any better for Izzy Inman. Besides, there was a possible murder story that was being handed to him on the proverbial silver platter. He hadn't felt as good since one of his columns led to the arrest, conviction and jail time for two Chicago aldermen, a host of precinct captains from the aldermen's wards and more fictitious pay rollers than in a Caspar the Friendly Ghost cartoon.

Riding in the passenger seat of the second Paddy Wagon was John Cinderella, the Junk Man. His son, Henry John was the Chicago Police officer driving the wagon to the courts at 26th and California. John had driven up in his junk trunk with a supply of used fire extinguishers he wanted to sell Bo. He got arrested instead.

Juan, Jorge, Jesus and Vincente, the valet parkers, followed in John Brown's BMW convertible. Juan gave his word to Noel that he wouldn't cut out of the procession as it sped to the courts at 26th and California. The BMW was sandwiched in between the first and second Paddy Wagons, the top down and music from a Latino station blaring out of the convertible while, the windshield wipers kept time to the music.

Bodies may have rattled around in the backs of the Paddy Wagons, but those bodies also had minds and those minds were creating alibis, and those alibis were logical, short and concise, each ending with, "I'm innocent."

> ***Naomi Schmitt was innocent because she helped the helpless and the homeless with her earnings.
>
> ***Peter and Pan used their pay to purchase kindergarten supplies, the rest being donated to the synagogue. They were innocent.
>
> ***Frank, Charles and Ramon did volunteer work comforting AIDS patients.
>
> ***Obadiah and Emerine were repentant sinners vowing to do the Lord's work of ridding the world of evil.
>
> ***Lucia Gunderson had come to save two of her students from a life of crime.
>
> ***Amanda Newton's main reason for being at La Tinkerbelle's was to save her one child. Secondary reasons centered on a rude phone call and the person or persons responsible for possibly harming her baby.
>
> ***Wanda Mensch came to La Tinkerbelle's out of curiosity. Before she knew it, she had slapped a police officer for calling her homely and asking her: "Could you be related in some way to Sid Mensch, Al Capone's old chef, the dumb ass

who used to make bath tub gin and sell it in the alley behind Scar Face's house?" Also, before she realized, she found herself falling in love with Bo Pepperwall.

As the collection of minds continued to concoct scenarios of innocence, the Paddy Wagons, sirens screaming, continued to make their way to 26th and California where a judge waited patiently. He too had read Izzy Inman's column.

John Brown awoke from unconsciousness to stare at a collection of what turned out to be an assortment of shoe soles. He was groggy, sore but a happy man. He hadn't been so happy since the day he scored the winning touchdown for his high school team's homecoming game his senior year. His happiness had continued after the game, when his scoring continued, this time with Susie Sansabar, the band's drum majorette and champion baton twirler. That night, in the back of team bus as it sat empty in the school parking lot, Susie gave John Brown baton twirling lessons he never forgot. Now John Brown would give all of his critics, his enemies and those he despised, lessons in the law they would never forget. "No one kicks me in the family jewels and gets away with it," he muttered to the rumble of the Paddy Wagon believing that no one heard him.

Arvia was beyond livid. She would find a way to make John Brown pay for having everyone who was a part of La Tinkerbelle's arrested, and she knew exactly how she would do it. After all, she was a Pepperwall, and Pepperwalls knew how to play dirty. They had invented the game, and Arvia had learned her lessons from a long line of dirty game players; the last one, not a Pepperwall, but her husband.

John Brown was wallowing in victory. Cocky and confident, even with a pain in the area of his groin that felt like the combined heels of the go-go boots worn by La Tinkerbelle's dancers had literally mashed his potatoes, he savored what he knew was a signed, sealed and delivered verdict of guilty on all counts. He was about to humble Mayor Arvia Pepperwall Bell and coerce her into doing things in a bedroom that were not designed for doing. "You're mine now, Ice Cube Lady," he thought. Get ready to watch the Master melt you." He tried to ignore the feel of boot heels and roller skate wheels digging into his spine as the Paddy Wagon's passengers stepped out into the parking area behind the court. He unceremoniously crawled out of the wagon and found himself sitting back on his haunches on the pavement wondering why there were no EMT's bringing him a wheelchair. "Come on, guys," he shouted at who he thought were three EMT's.

The Emergency Medical Technicians were behind the second Paddy Wagon talking Spanish to Juan and his valet parkers; the BMW parked in between the second and third Paddy Wagon. Laughter erupted from the group each time a head would turn in John Brown's direction.

"Where's my wheel chair," the lawyer shouted out. "Shake your lazy Spic asses."

The EMT's and parking valets ignored him.

"Hey, this is America," shouted the lawyer. "Speak English."

The group continued to speak in Spanish, laughing the entire time until a series of high fives took place and one of the EMT's pushed a wheelchair toward John Brown. "Your chariot has arrived," the EMT said to the attorney. "It's time to saddle up, amigo. Let me help you get your sorry gringo ass in the chair."

John Brown stood up and made a tentative move toward the wheelchair. Before he completed his first step, two pairs of hands had him under each arm and he found himself being dropped onto the seat. There was a flash and the agonizing feel of pain as the lawyer saw visions of knees arguing about who would hammer him in the groin next. Waiting patiently in line behind the knees were six pairs of white Go-Go boots, toes tapping in rhythm on the pavement. Behind them were the thigh high, vinyl black heels worn by Tinker Bell, Peter and Pan, stiletto heels taking practice aims while a phallic symbol hook hand clutching a conductor's baton led the dancing shoes.

"Your time is drawing near, John Brown," thought Arvia. She smiled as her mind reversed the obvious; arming her ducks with shotguns; lining them up while giving each a knowing nod as she set up her targets. John Brown would lead the way; her husband was second. A trio consisting of Alice Nell Puffin, Linda Ann Finn and Lucia Gunderson followed enhancing their unique walks with a series of bumps and grinds. Arvia pushed the *On* button and her parade of targets sauntered in a line from right to left, the sound of ratcheting gear teeth and clinking chains making music. When John Brown appeared in the bulls eye Arvia's ducks let loose with a deafening blast.

Arvia blinked. She didn't need a shooting gallery of ducks taking potshots at those who did her wrong. A special weapon awaited them, especially John Brown. Her weapon was evidence against the lawyer and that evidence came in several irrefutable forms. Arvia, with help from her secretary, Wanda Mensch, who never forgot the pain of writing thank you notes for political favors granted, those favors being delivered to his private steam room at the Glen Forest on the Watercourse Country Club. Quintin Bell referred to those deliveries as bonbons, brought in person by a variety curvaceous, luscious curiors minus any moral values.

The deliveries, as well as all of Mayor Bell's transactions—legal or illegal, right or wrong, good or evil—were kept in detail by Wanda Mensch during Quintin Bell's tumultuous tenure in office. Those transactions were joined by reams of copious notes taken by Wanda after observing John Brown and her boss in action and knowing the real reasons behind their actions. She knew what they had said about her, mocking her when they thought they were in private, making fun of her. Now it was her turn to flex her own muscles and her Mensa IQ. Wanda was more than happy to assist her new boss, Mayor Arvia Pepperwall Bell in making wrongs right.

As Arvia learned, her late husband and John Brown used the Mayor's political fund raising campaigns at the country club for their own personal gains. Funds got shifted and set aside for their personal pleasures. The campaign contributions followed a well camouflaged trail into Quintin Bell's secret bank account located, ironically enough, in a country where bon-bons of the highest quality were made. As Arvia discovered, with Wanda Mensch's pit bull tenacity, another account was located in a bank where gentle Caribbean breezes blew. The bank just so happened to be where Melvin White's retirement account sat with a one dollar balance. Thanks to the efforts of John Brown who Melvin White had hired at the suggestion of Quintin Bell, most of the late principal's ill-gotten beachcomber funds had been removed by John Brown in the form of maintenance fees. John Brown also received healthy stipends for his efforts laying paper trails that led to nowhere, the stipends coming in the form of many of Quintin Bell's well taped plain envelopes. "Surely, the Internal Revenue Service would be interested in that portion of unreported income on Mr. Brown's IRS 1040," said Arvia to Wanda.

"Indeed they would," replied Wanda. Her thin, pale lips spread into a wide grin. "And I'm just the one to plant a seed or two that would bring about an audit of one John Brown, Attorney-at-Law's finances."

Arvia agreed to Wanda's planting of a crop of evidence even though she possessed enough of her own, this collected without the help of Wanda Mensch. She silently smiled knowing she had several shovels of dirt to dump on the lawyer's grave, those in the form of: Sexual Abuse, Pornography and Statutory Rape; Bambi, his voluptuous secretary, was only seventeen.

On the one hand, Bo was thrilled that everyone including John Brown and his bruised testicles had escaped the fire. His dream had been destroyed but, for the first time in his life, he understood the meaning of self-worth. He didn't need Peter Pan or memories of his mother telling him what choices to make. His idol, Malcolm Forbes, didn't need calling on for help. He knew right from wrong and Berthold Bo Pepperwall knew who killed Quintin Bell. What better place than a court of law to announce to the whole world, at least the world of Glen Forest on the Watercourse and the tiny population of his Neverland called La Tinkerbelle's a Go-Go, who the murderer was. Bo never felt better. He was also in love with Wanda Mensch.

Judge Ransom Jones was not a happy man. If there was one facet of the Judge's life he cherished it was Monday afternoons with his cronies at Cronkite's Cigar Club. Ransom Jones was known as "Rans" or a number of other boyhood names that included, "Peanuts" referring to his size; "Salami" also referring to the size of a part of his anatomy and "Slaps" because he held his eighth grade graduating class record at St. Eulalia's School for being slapped more times at boy-girl parties for trying to cop a feel. Ransom Jones was born horny and went through life the same way having been married three times, the last time, when he turned sixty. His latest and current wife was a twenty nine year old bland court recorder who had very little in the line of anatomical curves but happened to be a nymphomaniac who would try anything in the bedroom. What cemented Ransom's desire for wedded bliss was the fact that his new bride used the most inappropriate filthy language to spur him to new sexual heights. Ransom Jones loved sexually explicit language; the dirtier the better, but not in his court and never inside the hallowed, sacred walls of Cronkite's. His Cronkite's cronies included several classmates from grammar school and high school and the rest a collection of lawyers, politicians, retired police captains and the politically connected. All of the Cronkite Cigar Club membership was white of hair, long in the tooth and should have frequented Comedy Clubs on Open Mike Night. Members of the media, including Izzy Inman, were black listed from Cronkite's and no cell phones were allowed in the smoke shrouded member's lounge. Cronkite's was filled with laughter, thick, aromatic cigar smoke and good natured teasing when the Monday meeting convened. Political correctness was also absent replaced by the overworked statement of: "I remember you when...."

This particular Monday afternoon, an hour or so before he was to leave for Cronkite's, Judge Jones received a last minute order to hear a case that only he was capable of hearing. He was not pleased. He sat brooding in his walnut paneled chambers psychologically preparing himself for the parade of liars, con artists, charlatans and "Alibi Ikes" as he referred to the defense attorneys he faced each day. He had similar derogatory names for the prosecution; not too many for most of the defendants and a few for wailing mothers who couldn't believe that they had given birth to a combined drug pusher, rapist and bank robber who wore women's clothing as a disguise. All Judge Ransom Jones knew was that he was going to be late for Cronkite's. He was not in a good mood.

Upon entering his full courtroom, Judge Jones's growing nasty disposition grew nastier. He hated full courtrooms. Full was not a new experience for the Judge. His courtroom demeanor, sarcastic sense of humor and verbal attacks at both the prosecution and the defense drew crowds of spectators. He couldn't believe what he saw before him from his seat on the bench. There wasn't a spectator in sight. His eyes scanned while his brain questioned. "Pirates wearing roller blades?" he muttered then blinking. "Two black cats?" he asked. There was another blink. "Eye patches?" He blinked three times when he saw Bo and thought, "What's that poor excuse for the captain of a garbage scow doing in here?" His knuckles attacked his eyes. "What the hell is this," he asked himself, "a Halloween party?" His gavel crashed down and he shouted, "Order!" One shout and one crash from Judge Ransom Jones was normally all it took to bring order in his court. This Monday afternoon he needed five and a second gavel after he broke the handle of the first on his third, "Order!" When silence finally came he looked around his courtroom until his eyes settled on one individual. Frustrated he asked, "Mildred, what in the hell are you doing in here?"

"I don't have a clue, younger brother," Mildred Farnsworth Pepperwall Jones replied savoring the moment. Another gavel bit the dust as what seemed like everyone in the courtroom interrupted Judge Jones and his sister with shouts of, "I'm innocent!" Singular cries of, "I'm ruined," that from Ramon to, "Bo, your nuts still belong to us," coming from Peter and Pan.

Just then the doors to the courtroom opened and the three Emergency Medical Technicians pushed in a wheel chair containing John Brown. Trailing behind the chair, dragging along the worn tile floor, was an oxygen mask, the mask connected to a tank that was turned on and hissing a foggy vapor. John Brown did not look well.

This was definitely not going to be a good day for Judge Jones.

"Your Honor," shouted Lucia Gunderson. "I put my life in jeopardy saving two of my most prized, innocent students from a life of white slavery," she said, her statement coming out with her New England lisp accent. "Why am I being arrested?"

The only part of Lucia Gunderson's interruption Judge Jones understood was about being arrested. Perhaps he would have paid more attention had he been aware of Lucia Gunderson's penchant for kinky sex sprinkled with lewd language.

"Your Honor," sang out Linda Ann Finn, her truncated impersonation of Barbra Streisand informing the court that she was the wife of Captain Mickey Finn, Chief of Police of the Glen Forest on the Watercourse. She quickly informed Judge Jones in a Key of C that she had accompanied her husband on his investigation of the secret dealings of Mayor Arvia Pepperwall Bell.

Judge Jones slammed down his gavel and heard the handle crack. The last thing he didn't need was Linda Ann Finn to detain him any longer from heading to Cronkite's.

Linda Ann Finn continued and so did Judge Jones. The top half of the Judge's second broken gavel cut her off in mid screech when it careened off his bench and landed in Linda Ann's open mouth.

The Judge disliked both Glen Forest on the Watercourse and Barbra Streisand. He disliked the town because a Mayor by the name of Quintin Bell had rejected his bid to reside there so he could be nearer his sister, Mildred. Besides, he liked his sister's traditional Sunday English Tea served with a strong belt of Gentleman Jack. He disliked the traffic clogging drive to see his sister and he also disliked Barbra Streisand because, after two divorces, it took forever for his happy days to become a part of his life again.

"Praise Jesus," shouted Pastor Rufus Puffin when seeing the top half of the judge's gavel plug Linda Ann Finn's mouth. "Praise the Lord," he shouted trying to get the Judge's attention as he raised a copy of the Bartender's Bible. His personal Holy Bible had been lost as he was being transported into the Paddy

Wagon and trying to protect his wife from the investigative hands of the arresting officers searching for concealed weapons. The pastor didn't notice that his wife enjoyed the searching.

"Jesus praised," muttered Judge Jones. "Moses too," he added.

"Senor Judge," said Juan Ponce de Leone politely. He was flanked by his parking lot attendants, all of them holding up their Green Cards. "We are legal citizens."

Judge Jones nodded.

Charles, being followed by Frank and Ramon, could no longer contain himself. He approached the bench as if he were a barrister from the United Kingdom. "Your, Grace," he stated eloquently. "My colleagues and I are pure and innocent of heart, mind and body and have committed no crimes against the Crown or you, your majestic Holiness." He winked. "Love that black robe. Is it a Lauren?"

Judge Jones's head went slowly from side to side, his eyes giving a silent order. In a second, a handful of bailiffs were leading the trio back to their seats, Charles stating to one of the bailiffs, "Unhand me, you silly savage." Then he began shouting, "Police brutality!" over and over until Frank plucked a plaid handkerchief with the cardboard bottom from the tux jacket of the nearest Cap'n's Kids band member, Regis and stuffed it in Charles's mouth.

Judge Jones's head continued going side to side.

"If it pleases the court, your honor," said John Brown from his wheel chair, his best courtroom demeanor and the chair not able to cover up his soot stained suit and the tattered area around his crotch. "John Horatio Brown, Attorney-at-Law. I'm responsible for bringing this collection of criminals to justice."

He did a slow wave of his hand from left to right in the direction of Bo, Arvia and the La Tinkerbelle's employees. He made another sweeping motion to be sure he included everyone else who got arrested including two undercover cops dressed as hookers who were on a stake-out in front of the housing project.

"You're responsible for this?" asked Judge Jones. His questions continued: "You? This? All of it?"

"Yes, your honor."

"All of this from that very wheel chair?" repeated the Judge. He looked squarely into the eyes of John Brown. "And just what is all of this, counselor?" the judge asked. "An Ironsides convention?"

John Brown was ready. His chance for revenge was now. Finally he could put to rest the likes of a Sam and his cats, Bo the Schmoe, carry out his plan to become Mayor of Glen Forest on the Watercourse and ravage the body of Arvia Pepperwall Bell. "Your honor," he started, and the charges flowed from him.

> ***No city, county and state business licenses.
> ***No liquor license.
> ***No insurance of any kind.
> ***Violation of EPA, city, county and state laws against the dumping of hazardous waste.
> ***Endangering and contributing to the delinquency of minors.

"That's what I was trying to tell you, Judge!" lisped Lucinda Gunderson in a shout.

The Judge's right index finger waved gently about an inch from side to side.

John Brown welcomed the interruption. He smiled at Bo, his

smile saying, "See, I told you so." He continued on enumerating, according to him, dastardly, malicious deed after dastardly, malicious deed.

***No pet licenses and cruelty to those same pets.

***Violation of the Mann Act.

***Pornographic movies and charging a fee for the viewing of same.

***Displaying and selling adult oriented materials without a license.

***Mislabeling and misrepresenting the portions of alcoholic beverages being sold.

"That's a lie, you two-bit shyster," replied Sam, over John Brown's voice. "Just as it's a lie that my guys were being treated with cruelty."

The judge's index finger began to wave again much to the pleasure of John Brown.

"If you want examples of cruelty, Your Honor," continued Sam, ignoring the judge's finger, "that cancerous growth on the breast of the legal profession, that embarrassment to lawyers everywhere and sexual abuser of women...."

"I object, your honor," said John Brown. "I'm not on trial here."

"Am I on trial?" asked Mildred Farnsworth Pepperwall Jones to her grandson, Noel.

"Kind of, Grandma," said Noel, nodding sheepishly. "You're kind of being arraigned."

"Oh, goody," she said.

"Am I on trial too?" asked Wanda Mensch. "The only crime I committed was to do the Bunny Hop and help Berthold save all of those people from being burned alive in that terrible fire."

"Bunny Hop," repeated the Judge.

"And that's the reason why I'm pressing charges against this entire cast of hallucinogenic characters, these dregs of society who possess, in toto, not one ounce of social redeeming value," stated an eloquent John Brown. He looked at Bo and pointed. "This loser," he said, his professional demeanor showing signs of unraveling as the two Tylenol the EMT's had given him for the pain in his groin were wearing off, "was responsible for a multitude of building code violations that contributed to that disastrous conflagration that could have killed more human beings than the historic tragedy of Chicago's Iroquois Theatre fire. Almost everyone in this courtroom was employed by one Berthold Bo Pepperwall of Glen Forest on the Watercourse and contributed in some part to those violations. Mr. Pepperwall knew of those violations and ignored those violations. So did his employees." He paused, his confidence returned. "Bo Pepperwall is not a hero, your honor he's a villain, a criminal, a heinous monster of the highest order." "At least I'm not a murder," retorted Bo, stepping forward, buttoning the two remaining buttons that remained on his captain's jacket.

Judge Jones's white hair seemed to get whiter and thinner as he looked down from the bench over the tops of his glasses pinching the end of his nose. To expedite the hearing and to get to Cronkite's, Judge Jones ordered the bailiffs to group the defendants and place them in clusters of ten, lined up like bowling pins in front of his bench. He ended up with three full groups and a fourth minus the seven and ten pins. Even the two undercover cop/prostitutes were racked up.

CLICK/SNAP.

Judge Jones glared at Bo.

Bo slid his lighter slowly into a torn pants pocket of his Captain's uniform.

Judge Jones glanced at the sheaf of papers in front of him and then returned to staring at Bo. "A very impressive list of violations, Mister Pepperwall," he said, looking at the papers again and then at Bo, repeating the process several times. "Let me see. No smoke detectors, no sprinkler system, and blocked fire exits." What sounded like a deep groan came from his throat.

"Your honor," Bo shouted, his entire body appearing agitated. "Mr. Brown blocked the rear fire exit by his callous and cowardly behavior."

"Your honor," interrupted John Cinderella, the junk man, "I was dropping off Mr. Pepperwall's order for fire extinguishers when I was arrested."

"Judge, Sir, your Honor" called out Ben. "I was just sipping root beer. My Uncle Bo gets the best root beer from Wisconsin."

"Root beer," repeated a puzzle Judge Jones, as if he were talking to his cronies at Cronkite's. "What does root beer have to with these criminal charges?" The judge continued to stare at Bo. "And, look, Mr. Pepperwall, no liquor license, and no building permits for remodeling and no Board of Health inspection for the restaurant, and no insurance." He shook his head and said, "None whatsoever." His head shook again and said, "Very good, Mr. Pepperwall. Tell me, were you ever hit in the head with a croquet mallet when you were a young child?"

"I earned my doctorate from the University of Chicago when I was sixteen," said Bo, with a shrug. "But I did see my brother-in-law get killed with a croquet mallet."

Judge Jones shook his head and looked at Bo. "You got your

doctorate when you were sixteen?" he asked.

Arvia nodded at the judge. "He did, your Honor," she said. "My brother's brilliant. "He belongs to Mensa."

"Really," muttered the Judge. "Did you say Mensa or mental?"

"You belong to Mensa?" asked Wanda Mensch, looking up at Bo with more than admiration. "I do too."

Judge Jones's head went from side to side and he said, "Normally, my court is full of idiots with no brains. Now I have two people in here who have more brains than all of the criminals, thugs and societal misfits of the earth who have ever graced my chambers. And I'm not even counting the politicians." He looked at Amanda Newton and Arvia and crossed his index fingers together and said, "What were you two ladies thinking about? Were you really suspended from wires, swinging across a crowded room?" he asked. He paused then, his voice boomed out: "Nude and in front of your children?"

"Your Honor," Amanda began to say.

Judge Jones put is index finger to his lips. "No, no, no. Even if you are a school librarian, I don't want to hear it." He glared at Amanda. "If you want to talk in here it will cost you a fine of two cents." He held up his left hand, the index and middle fingers spread apart. "Otherwise, silence, please."

Ben and Matilda turned fiery red.

Judge Jones glanced at Arvia. "And, you, Mrs. Bell, do you behave like that in your role as Mayor or in any other role for that matter, in your prestigious suburban community?"

"Your Honor, I can." Arvia never got a chance to explain.

Judge Jones's index finger stayed glued to his lips. "Please,

Mrs. Bell, no excuses. You are, I believe, the Mayor of your community?"

Arvia nodded.

The judge's eyes settled on the third row and he looked at Peter, Matilda and Pan and said, "And as for you three young ladies. I'm a patron of the arts, but Tinker Bell and Peter and Pan? Oh, Mary Martin, where are you now that we need you?"

Peter, Pan and Matilda lowered their eyes.

Then Judge Jones's eyes focused in on the last row at Frank, Charles, Ramon, Ben, Sam and the two cats. "You hindered the fire fighters from doing their job with the Bunny Hop? Is that correct, the Bunny Hop?"

Frank tried to explain starting with, "But, Your Honor." He never got in another word.

Judge Jones's shook his head.

Charles ignored the Judge's request to keep silent. "We weren't hindering, Your Majesty. We were getting people away from the scene and to safety so they wouldn't panic and get hurt or, worse yet, get killed. No one was injured because of the Bunny Hop, Your Grace."

"We also had the crowd doing The Stroll and the Watusi across the parking lot," Obadiah yelled out. "I even got their attention with my championship Arkansas hog call. Wanna hear it, Judge?"

Judge Jones's head barely budged from side to side and he gently tapped the broken handle of his gavel. "No hog calls, please." He looked at Charles. "And, Sir, I am not Your Majesty."

Charles was flustered. "Well, you know what I meant, Your Excellency."

The judge rolled his eyes and looked at Ben. "And, you, young man, what is someone your age doing in a topless bar besides drinking root beer?"

It wasn't topless your Honor," said Ben. "I was only helping my..."

The judge rolled his eyes again. "Excuses, excuses," he muttered. "I'm tired of excuses. The head phones, young man. Remove them."

"Sorry Your Honor," said Ben, as he pulled the plugs from his ears. "Gosh, you're just like my mom."

"Thank you for the compliment, young man," said Judge Jones's. "And your mother is?"

"The Mayor, Your Honor," replied Ben politely.

"Good job, Mayor Mom," he said to Arvia, as he then turned his attention to Sam and his two cats. "Weren't you in my court once before?"

"Yes, Your Honor," said Sam, as Heckle purred in his right hand and Jeckle in his left.

"That's what I thought," said the Judge. "Never forget a face or a case, especially one with two cats. John Brown kind of nailed you to the cross that day." The Judge paused and glanced at his wrist watch. Cronkite's was still a distinct possibility. "I guess you learned you can't represent yourself in a court of law." He paused, his head shaking from side to side. "Not against a couple of heavyweights like Mr. Brown here and that late mayor fellow." He paused, thinking. "Ah, Quintin Bell, that's who the other guy was; a ruthless son of a gun." He thought for a moment. "Ruthless on the football field as well as I recall. Wasn't his nickname, Ding Dong, Mr. Brown? That's when he used to block for you. Hit those other guys so hard all they heard was ding dong when they hit the turf. Anyone could've made All-American with Ding Dong blocking for them. Heck, I thought he should've won the Heisman." He glanced at John Brown. "Here you are again, Mr. Brown, all by your lonesome and in a wheel chair. Aren't you afraid of all of these people without that Quintin Bell fellow running interference for you?"

John Brown was ready for Judge Jones's remark. "We're not on the gridiron, Your Honor," he said softly, keeping his blood from boiling at the judge's comment about making All-American. "I have nothing to fear in a court of law."

"Not even a croquet mallet?" mutter Bo loud enough for the court room to hear.

"Amen to that," whispered Naomi Schmitt way too loud.

"I agree with y'all," came from Alice Nell Puffin's southern drawl. "Croquet mallets can be so much fun when it the right hands, but, sheeeet, they're also dangerous."

"Most definitely fun," lisped Lucia Gunderson.

"And deadly," said Amanda Newton

"Enough," said the judge appearing disgusted. He looked at John Brown. "Okay, counselor, you've pressed your charges. Is there anything else?"

John Brown saw his opening as if he were carrying a football off tackle. He nodded his appreciation to the judge. "Your Honor, I'm here to represent Mrs. Bell."

The judge did a double take. "You're pressing charges against this lady and now you're representing her. Make up your mind."

"I'm offering my services pro bono, Your Honor."

"That's big of you, Mr. Brown, said Judge Jones. "I'm sure

that one of the swinging nude mothers thanks you."

"The heck you are," Arvia spurted out, inching her way to John Brown. "Over my dead body," she hissed.

"Whoa now," said Judge Jones, looking at John Brown. "Did you say you're representing Mrs. Bell?"

"I did, Your Honor."

"Didn't you work with a Quintin Bell in this here very court against that guy standing over there?" Judge Jones pointed at Sam. "What did you two refer to him as?" The judge paused. "Oh, now I remember. Geronimo Germono, the gay pervert. Isn't that right, Counselor?"

Amanda Newton gasped.

Mildred Farnsworth Pepperwall Jones let out a tiny giggle.

Wanda Mensch lowered her head to cover her smile.

Ramon, Charles and Frank joined hands.

John Brown nodded and said, "Your Honor has a keen memory."

"You two bozos got a building or a bar or something like that from this here, Sam fella."

"Well Your Honor," said John Brown, ready to deliver his explanation.

"Save it, Counselor," said Judge Jones, glancing again at his watch and then at the crowded gallery when he spotted Regis, Reggie and Rommie. "Excuse me, gentlemen, but the last time I saw anyone wearing tuxes like that was in *Forever Plaid*. You guys related to My Cousin Vinnie?"

Reggie said politely, "Well Your Honor, let me explain."

Judge Jones waved his index finger at Reggie. "Didn't you gentlemen used to play with the Sammy Kaye orchestra?" he asked. "Late forties or early fifties; at The Sherman House;

College Inn? Am I Right?"

"That's right, Judge," said Rommie joining the conversation. "We were still in our teens then."

"That's what I thought," said Judge Jones. "My parents had fond memories of going to see you play way back when. Tell me, gentlemen, are things really that tough in show biz that you took a job in a topless bar?"

Rommie shrugged, "Well Your Honor, at our age and living on Social Security, a gig's a gig, man."

"I hope things look up for you gentlemen," said Judge Jones, as his eyes traveled to Obadiah and Emerine.   "And what do you folks do?"

Obadiah suppressed the urge to let out a hog call and said: "We're rock singers, Judge. And we got married today."

"And repentant sinners," Your Honor," Emerine added.

"Amen," Pastor Puffin also added.

The Judge glanced around his court room.   "I've got an octogenarian rock band, bunny hoppers, defendants dressed up like refugees from the Artist's and Model's Ball and two black cats. Oh, and I almost forgot, there's Izzy Inman from the Daily Examiner."   The judge nodded in Izzy Inman's direction. "Good column this morning. Did those two no-talent celebrity idiots get married?"

Izzy smiled and nodded.

The judge looked puzzled, and then he looked at Obadiah and Emerine. "Are you two the newlyweds mentioned in Izzy's column?" he asked, but didn't wait for an answer. Time was getting away from him and so was Cronkite's. He looked around his courtroom. "And who may I ask married you?"

"Reverend Rufus McDowell Puffin, Pastor of the United

Church of the Glen, Your Honor," said Rufus Puffin who was again sweating profusely.

"I take it the newlyweds had city and state licenses," said Judge Jones.

"The good Lord doesn't require a license to bring two people together in Holy Matrimony," said Rufus, his Scottish accent put on display.

"Seems to be a lot of that going around nowadays," said the judge, as he glanced at Sam again. "Did I really allow Mr. Brown and that Bell fellow to take your business from you?"

Sam nodded.

"Shame on me, Sam," he said apologetically. "But, the law's the law."

"Your Honor," said Arvia, ignoring Judge Jones's waving index finger. "My late husband and Mr. Brown were wrong for what they did. But, I own that property now, the entire strip shopping mall, and I'm sure something can be worked out to make things right for Sam." She turned and smiled at Sam.

John Brown took a step forward. "If it pleases the court Your Honor?"

"It doesn't," said the Judge. "But, go ahead. Earn your keep."

"Mrs. Bell is still a bit shaken from the terrible ordeal she has just experienced. As her attorney...."

Arvia approached the bench stepping in front of John Brown in his wheel chair. As she did her right foot kicked him in his ankle. "Your Honor is there some way..." she nodded at John Brown. "You can get him to shut up?"

"He's a lawyer," said the Judge. "I guess I could have him shot."

"Your Honor," said Arvia pleading. "This is all a big misunderstanding made even worse by Mr. Brown. Regardless of what the charges are I can tell you that Bo never dumped toxic waste from the factory into the Chicago River. He thought about it."

CLICK/SNAP.

Judge Jones glared at Bo. " One more game of imitating a cricket from you Mr. Pepperwall, and you'll be hearing the clank clink of contempt of court when that jail cell door slams shut on you."

Arvia continued. "And my brother listened to Sam's advice about not filling up the empty, name liquor bottles with cheap substitutes."

The Judge scanned the pages in front of him. "Interesting," he said. "Did I miss something?"

"No matter," said Arvia. "He didn't do any such thing. I mean, Mr. Brown accused him of using mystery meat in the restaurant for our special gourmet meat loaf, but my brother didn't. The chef wouldn't let him."

"Oh, that's a comforting thought," said Judge Jones, the faint smell of intoxicating cigar smoke testing his senses.

Arvia continued defending her brother. "And, as for the little forgery incident, Bo and I worked that out."

"Forgery?" asked the judge, showing a spark of interest in the discussion. "I don't see that listed here either."

"It was a loan Your Honor." said Arvia.

"Your Honor," said John Brown, an arrogant defiance in his voice. "I...."

Like a lightning strike, Arvia turned and slapped John Brown. Even the bailiffs felt her hand.

Judge Jones gently tapped the broken handle of his gavel and smiled. "Well, I guess that's one way to shut a lawyer up."

"Your Honor," said Sam, politely addressing the judge. "I'd like to say something in defense of Mr. Pepperwall."

The judge gave his shoulders a shrug. "Why not," he said. "The man needs all the defenses he can get."

"Your Honor," continued Sam. "When the business, well, when there wasn't any business, Mr. Pepperwall could have sent us all home, but he kept everyone on the payroll. I mean, there were no cars to park, but Juan and his boys got paid. And so did the waiters and waitresses, and more than minimum."

Obadiah raised his hand. "Judge, Sir, I'd also like to add that Pepperwalls donated food and clothes to some of the needy families in the neighborhood. Even when there was no business, like Sam just said, he donated clothes from the boutique and food from the kitchen."

Naomi Schmitt nervously twirled her artificial hook, switching hands. "Your Honor, Mr. Pepperwall also paid me when only a handful of customers came to La Tinkerbelle's. I used that money to help establish a new clinic."

"A belly dancing clinic?"

"No, Your Honor," she said. "My real name is Naomi Schmitt. I'm a social worker and I work with the elderly and with babies who are addicted to crack cocaine. I lost my clinic when Sam lost his bar. We were in the same building. When Mr. Pepperwall hired me he paid me way too much for what I do, but with that money he gave me I could continue helping the elderly and those sick babies."

"Excuse me, Judge," said Juan. "But I would like to say something about Senor Bo."

"Why not?" replied Judge Jones, taking a quick look at his watch. "Everyone else is. Go ahead, Senor."

"Well, Judge," said Juan. "Senor Bo bought uniforms for our parish little league baseball program. Not just uniforms for one team, Judge, but uniforms for every kid on every team.

Gracias, Senor Judge." Juan stepped back, walked to Bo and shook his hand.

Frank and Charles started to step forward with Charles saying to the Judge, "Your Royal Highness I...."

Frank moved in front of Charles giving him a slight shove to the side. "What my partner wants to say Your Honor is that Mr. Pepperwall did mislead our customers as to the authenticity of our merchandise. He's guilty of that.

CLICK/SNAP.

"But, he stopped when we told him he was wrong," continued Frank.

"And, My Lord," continued Charles, he took a major percentage of those profits and made a more than generous donation to our request for Aids Research. Charles approached the bench, walked behind it, and pinned a small red ribbon on the Judge's robe just before the bailiff, a brawny handsome, dark skinned man, escorted him back to where he was. Charles smiled at him. "Support the cause, your Majesty. And you too, he said" to the bailiff as he stroked the stripes of his rank on his sleeve.

"Anyone else who...."

"Your honor, Sir," said Matilda as she timidly approached the bench.

"Alright, young lady, everyone else in the menagerie has had something to say, what's on your mind?"

"This was my entire fault Your Honor," said Matilda. "I mean, all I wanted to do was to show my mother that I could do something besides catalogue books in the library. My friend, Ben, he tried." She stopped and turned indicating Ben should join her. "Ben's my boyfriend and he tried to talk me out of working for his uncle, Mr. Pepperwall. But if I didn't work for him, I would've never met my father. I would have never met Peter and Pan and never met Frank and Charles."

"And me," interrupted Ramon.

Matilda smiled at Ramon. "I know what I did was wrong," she said, taking Ben's hand. "And I didn't want to hurt anyone especially my mother. It was Mrs. Bell who tried to keep my mother from swinging out over the audience to cover me up." She put her hands to her face for a moment. "I didn't know that part of my mother's clothes had been torn off."

Ben put a comforting arm around her shoulder.

"Thank you, young lady," said Judge Jones. "And thank all of you for presenting the facts to this court." He shuffled the papers in front of him, signed a page and then put the papers into a file folder. "Mr. Pepperwall, the way I see it, I should have you incarcerated, fine you and send you to another country where they would cane you within an inch of your life. When that part of your sentence was completed I should have you exiled to Devil's Island." He paused, shook his head in frustration, glanced at his watch and saw there was still time to join his friends at Cronkite's. "Ah, why don't you just pay a few fines and all of you get out of my sight. His broken gavel made a poor excuse for a bang and he said, "Before I render my decision," he said, "I've really got to hear who killed Mayor Quintin Bell."

CHAPTER 7

Glen Forest, Buck Town, Sedona and Minocqua

(Where the Flowers Went)

Nostalgia swarmed over Bo coating him like the sticky, gooey weather that did more that stifle him at his brother-in-law's funeral a few short months ago. He was leaving Dogwood. His coach house womb would soon be gone forever, his sister having leased the family estate. The life he knew, one filled with safety and security, albeit frustrating and demeaning, was being swapped like one of his ancestral General's deals. This new venture was filled with uncertainty, passion and the love of Wanda Mensch.

He glanced at the yellowed dresser mirror and saw Malcolm Forbes grinning back at him as if to say, "Berthold, you sly dog." Then he thought he saw the picture wink.

Bo carefully removed the dog eared picture from the mirror and gave it one last look. He saw the open black plastic garbage bag with the yellow pull strings on top of his bare, stained mattress. The bag yawned wide. Bo put the picture inside the bag being careful not to crease it. His fingers yanked the yellow pull ties shut then knotted them. There was one last glance around what he had known as home since his mother died and his sister met Quintin Bell. He shut off the light, heard the click of the door behind him and headed down the coach house's wooden stairs concealed behind the garage.

Hans greeted him with a click of his heels, a slight bow and a disciplined look that was given away by smiling blue eyes. He took the plastic bag, and as Bo had instructed him earlier, placed it in one of the plastic trash containers alongside the garage. Hans, too, was in a new phase of his life. His mind was still trying to decipher the series of events that had started outside the courthouse at 26th and California in the back parking lot. Lucia Gunderson had introduced herself and offered to give him a ride back to Glen Forest on the Watercourse in the little yellow school bus. At that instant, his life changed forever. Along with her friends, Lucia took Hans to the school bus that was still parked on the street in front of La Tinkerbelle's, the flashing lights still on and the stop sign arm extended out. Confusing Hans was the fact that he found himself attracted to Lucia Gunderson. The last itme he had feelings like this for a woman was when he was a physical fitness instructor back in Germany. Those feelings were for the assistant gymnastic's instructer, Heidi Messerschmidt. Heidi, after hours in the gyn when the two of them closed up at night, showed him floor exercise moves he never knew were part of gymnastics. Hans was the floor in Heidi's demonstrations.

As if in a delirious daze, Hans went from the court to a yellow school bus to the Principal's office and the top of her desk wondering if Eva Braun went after the Fuehrer as fast as Lucia did him. At least he now knew what the word, blitzkrieg meant. He did, however, have his doubts that Eva yodeled during love making; especially with a lisp and using erotic yodels. After hours of erotic sex in the principal's office doing things he had discovered while cleaning the men's room stalls of La Tinkerbelle's, all he could say was, "You Scandinavian Nymphomanin, ich liebe Dich." Hans's ignited passion was led by Lucia to her apartment where they never saw daylight for a week. Memories of Heidi Messerschmidt vanished.

There was an interlude where Hans showed Lucia his Dogwood guardhouse and introduced her to Schickle and Gruber. He knew that any woman who could sing German beer drinking songs and wanted him to wear his highly polished knee boots during sex would be his wife. Besides, he thought, her orgasmic screams probably reverberated all the way to the Alps.

Lucia Gunderson had become more than intrigued with Hans after he almost knocked her off the metal platform of Le Tinkerbelle's while spinning Bo Pepperwall around on his shoulders. "He's thyice da hunk or Myer Bell" she had stated to Linda Ann Finn in her New England lobster pot accent. "An, dowed you see dem boots gristen in da zoanlight?"

Lucia Gunderson had wasted no time introducing herself to Hans when she got to the parking lot behind the courts. "You are the bweevest beeny hoper I have eber seen," she lisped, her right hand extended out.

Everyone in the back parking lot of the courts had been met by Officers Peccarino and Jones who had offered to drive them back to La Tinkerbelle's to retrieve their vehicles. Bouncing around in the back of the Paddy Wagon in a series of half on and half off of Hans's lap, Lucia found herself more than intrigued with Hans. She was falling in love. Bouncing on Hans's lap in the back of the Paddy Wagon also made the principal incredibly horny.

Several weeks later and on the brink of sexual exhaustion, Lucia shared with her new love a secret filled with guilt. During their drowsy periods of relaxing after love making, Lucia related to Hans how she had left him while he slept on two occasions to run errands. The errands, as it turned out, had been to John Brown's attorney's office. The first trip was the presentation of a proposition by John Brown's attorney. The second trip was for Lucia to pick up a sizeable check. The check was her not coming forward with damning photographic evidence she possessed of her and John Brown. It seems that Quintin Bell had sent John Brown with the legal agreement spelling out Lucia Gunderson's appointment as the new principal of the Glen Forest on the Watercourse High School. There were no clauses in the contract stipulating or regulating appropriate or inappropriate behavior on the party of the first part, Lucia Gunderson and the party of the second part, John Brown. Lucia's new office and her old aquarium received the brunt of the passion. A hidden camera in the principal's office recorded a session worthy of viewing in the men's room of the now defunct La Tinkerbelle's a Go-Go. The hush money Lucia received consisted, in part, of John Brown's cut from Quintin Bell's bon-bon candygram deliveries. John Brown was going away for a long time. Pictures of him and Lucia, along with Alice Nell Puffin, Linda Ann Finn and Bambi, his underage secretary, would have made his time away much longer had the photographs and DVD's had not been withheld as evidence.

"And, dat mine honey boney hoper, is da trut," she had told Hans. Before he could comment, Lucia sternly ordered, "Now click der heals of doze boots, you stud."

Hans, thanks to Lucia and John Brown, now had his own

limousine company. He was a company of one stretch limo and one driver, him, and an address that was still Dogwood, as it also continued to be for Schickle and Gruber. He and Lucia had entered into a lease agreement with Arvia. They would be caretakers of Dogwood with the intent of opening the grounds for paid visitors' tours and turning a section of the mansion into a Bed and Breakfast, Dogwood having been given historical landmark status. Lucia would also board and breed dogs, converting an area behind the swimming pool and tennis courts into her kennel/pet hotel. She planned to breed German Sheppard stock using Schickle and Gruber. All Lucia Gunderson had to do in her arrangement with Arvia was to step down as principal of the high school and turn over the reins to Amanda Newton. As Lucia discovered, Arvia also had pictures of her.

The limousine's trunk lid was lashed down with a series of crisscrossed bungee cords securing the steamer trunk and two large suitcases once belonging to Quintin Bell; all courtesy of Bo's sister. The matching luggage was packed with Quintin Bell's now altered clothes, custom tailored by Giovanni the tailor to fit Bo Pepperwall. Giovanni couldn't do a thing for Bo's shoes but Bo didn't care. He liked the feel of his feet swimming around in custom, handmade calf skin originals.

Bo had said his good-byes to his sister, wishing her well, and saying: "I can't see you living in a condo after a life in Dogwood but Officer Peccarino seems like a good guy."

"He's more than a good guy," said Arvia. She had surprised her brother and the entire of Glen Forest on the Watercourse community by resigning the Mayor's position and naming as her replacement, Raphael "Rip" Repeater, the trusted, no nonsense grounds keeper of the country club.   Rip's appointment had no challenges.   His cache of memorabilia of Quintin Bell's fund raisers was safely locked away in some hide-a-way known possibly only by a Hernando or an Ali Baba. Arvia had wanted Officer Peccarino to move to her mansion, but as he quickly pointed out, he would lose his job and his pension with the Chicago Police Department because he no longer met the City of Chicago residency requirement. Those were the rules and, unlike her late husband and a long line of Pepperwalls who had never met a rule they didn't bend or break, her new love was first and foremost an officer of the law. She didn't bother to tell him that she had more money than the entire Chicago Police Department had in its pension fund.

Arvia didn't hesitate with Officer Peccarino's invitation to move in with him into Buck Town. She loved the intimacy of the near northwest side of Chicago condo, the snugness of the neighborhood with its mix of ethnicity, quaint shops and trendy bistros, and all within walking distance.   Besides, with the money that her brother and late husband never saw or knew existed, she bought up the entire block of old, charming homes across the street in need of rehab. It was the ideal project for her.

Bo was happy for her. He was also happy for Sam who had finally gotten his old life back with Amanda and his Princess Matty.   Amanda, after Arvia had accepted Lucia Gunderson's resignation, accepted the offer to become the new principal of Glen Forest on the Watercourse High School.   She would continue to live in her apartment above Shake's Mortuary. After graduation, Matilda would stay in Chicago and attend either Loyola or DePaul majoring in theater while Ben would matriculate to Northwestern. The two college freshmen were within a short El train ride to either campus. Ben, to his surprise, discovered that Matilda had waved her two cents price tag for him.

Ramon, thanks to several follow-up articles in Izzy Inman's column and several free hair pieces, saw his salons blossom into a chain across the country. Charles managed the western half of the United States while Frank the east. The west coast was totally suited to Charles's life style and nothing he did or said, no one he bit, not a soul he groped, cared. Frank loved New York and he took a giant size bite out of the apple. Not the same as the bites Charles was gouging out along the west coast. They talked non-stop on their cell phones, texting until their thumbs were almost stumps and even Skyping, but they never saw each other again in person and Frank couldn't have been happier.

Rufus Puffin returned to Aberdeen without Alice Nell. He took over a vacant country church hidden among the Scottish countryside and, although he had only a handful of farm families as parishioners, he provided spiritual guidance to the farmers in luxurious comfort thanks to his share of a settlement for the pictures he possessed of his wife and John Brown.

Alice Nell moved to Sedona, Arizona with Linda Ann Finn who left her Chief of Police husband, Mickey, for a new, exciting and sometimes provocative life. The two ladies had bought a vacated lodge that had been used for spiritual rejuvenation rituals with emphasis on magnetic healing of the psyche and the sweating out of evil spirits. More hush money from John Brown's attorney got credit for their acquisition. Happy days were definitely back for Alice Nell and Linda Ann especially with Alice Nell giving Linda Ann a standing ovation each time she did her impersonation of Barbra Streisand.

Cubbie and Davia, aka Peter and Pan, returned to their kindergarten students. Their desire to neuter Bo Pepperwall was quickly forgotten by bonuses paid to them by Bo. The two were reading specialists, but vowed never to have a copy of Peter Pan in their classroom. The money they made in their brief careers in show business coupled with the generous bonuses they received allowed them to stay kindergarten teachers. They had paid off their student loans, bought real furniture, gave a generous donation to the rabbi and never ate Wheaties and water again.

Noel Jones continued his weekly visit to his grandmother in Glen Forest on the Watercourse delivering her ration of Gentleman Jack. Periodically, he would volunteer to help Naomi Schmitt in her social work with senior citizens. He turned down every offer from Naomi to pay him for his services, donating, instead, a substantial part of a discrete settlement he had received from John Brown's attorney. Noel Jones quickly became an aficionado of Middle Eastern dancing, including lap versions, in the privacy of his or Naomi's apartment.

What Sam and Bo suddenly realized was they were neighbors; Sam back with his former wife and Bo engaged to and living with Wanda Mensch. One morning they met while taking out the garbage at the base of the wooden staircase behind Shakes. Sam spoke first saying, "So that was your voice I've been hearing through the wall at night," he said smiling. "My, my, Captain, but I didn't know that you were the ultimate shiverer of timbers."

Bo blushed then said to Sam, "Me thinkest you do more than speak with forked tongue, Geronimo."

They tried to hide their smiles by looking into their stained brown paper garbage bags. It was Sam, eyes smiling, who looked up and asked: "Do you remember that group of college kids we tossed out of Le Tinkerbelle's?"

Bo nodded, smiled and said, "Rude little finger pointing snot noses as I recall." His smile disappeared. "Thought they knew it all; even telling us that they knew where all go-go's had gone."

"And having the nerve to call us old and that we sucked," Sam quickly pointed out. He smiled and gave a shrug almost spilling out part of the garbage from his bag. "They kind of reminded me of how I was when I was their age. He looked at Bo, his eyes beaming. "Go-Go's were gone-gone by then but I heard all about them from my mother. She also told me where all the flowers had gone and that no one ever learned a thing back then." He paused and re-gripped his garbage. Suddenly, Sam surprised Bo by asking, "I was wondering," he started out, his eyes uncharacteristically darting back and forth as he if he were afraid to go on, "where did you ever lay your hands on that old, relic of a Zippo lighter you used to click and snap all the time?"

Bo gave Sam a puzzled look. "Gee, I don't know," he replied, his Mensa mind whirling. "My mother gave it to me just before she died. She told me she got it at some flea market while on vacation with my father in Minocqua, Wisconsin. That was just before my father ran off with some cabaret singer and left me and my sister with Mom." He gave Sam a questioning look but didn't ask.

"My mother had a lighter like that," Sam said softly, almost reverently. "It was part of my father's personal belongings."

It was Bo's turn to give the questioning look.

"My dad was killed in Viet Nam when I was an infant. The government gave my mother his dog tags, a Zippo lighter with his outfit engraved on it and an American flag."

Bo nodded, trying to understand.

"Obviously, I never knew my dad but, as I got older, my mother told me more and more about him," he said, re-gripping his garbage bag. "She held off on the war stuff until just before she died." He closed his eyes, thought and then continued. "My dad must've gone through hell over in those jungles and rice paddies. When I realized what he had experienced; the slaughter and the carnage, I knew that whatever I would encounter in my life couldn't come close to what he lived over there."

"All I know about what happened during that time is what I read about," said Bo, re-gripping his garbage bag.

Sam nodded, his bag being shifted to the opposite arm. "My mom let me sort of play with the lighter. I would click it and snap it just like you," he said, then pausing and smiling before continuing. "But I wasn't as maniacal as you." He continued to smile. "When I held that scarred lighter in my hands I swear I could feel my father's spirit; feel his strength. It was as if he was trying to make me strong." Sam glanced down. "It was as if he knew that I would be going into my own form of combat with a sadistic enemy. I never knew an enemy could be named Bell and Brown."

"I like the word, sadistic," replied Bo, feeling a growing respect for his friend.

"I guess Dad knew that his son would someday be facing his own carnage and living out of a shopping cart. He was preparing me for scrounging for food in garbage cans." He stopped and gave his garbage bag a squeeze almost forcing some of the contents to spill over the top of the bag.

A sad look engulfed Bo. "Sam, I had a doctorate at sixteen and I didn't know a thing. My world was one of Peter Pan, Tinker Bell, Captain Hook and Smee. Like you I only heard about discotheques and go-go bars. I saw pictures of them. Had I have been old enough to experience a place like a discotheque I wouldn't have been able to go. I never had any money to go to any places like that. My mother kept me broke. Later, so did my brother-in-law, your buddy the mayor. I ended up going through life with nothing but lint in my pockets." His smile broadened into a grin. "At least those kids we threw out of La Tinkerbelle had money in the wallets we lifted from them."

Sam nodded. "And false ID cards; even a hot credit card or two," he said, then pausing, a serious look covering his face. "I kind of got the feeling that's how your late brother-in-law and John Brown must've felt after taking away everything from me."

"And, did you believe the potty mouth on that one girl?" asked Bo, trying to change the subject. "My, oh, my," he muttered.

Sam broke into a laugh. "Kind of like what I hear coming through our bedroom wall at night."

Bo turned red. "Time to take out the garbage," he said.

For years, Wanda Mensch had been a slave to her job and her fantasies. Now she had more than a make-believe life. She was in love with Berthold Bo Pepperwall. Gone were her days of longing to be Wendy and aching to be ravished by Quintin Bell.

While waiting in the court's back parking area after being turned loose by Judge Jones, she had invited Bo to join her for coffee at Mildred's Ennui Latte Emporium when they got back to Glen Forest on the Watercourse.

Bo had accepted her invitation before she had a chance to attempt a flutter of her lash-less eyelids.

Bo, never having money for anything, let alone trendy coffee, sipped a cup of cappuccino courtesy of Wanda. He couldn't take his eyes off of her tongue that seemed to dart in and out of her bourbon laced coffee like a hummingbird savoring a flower's nectar. "Is Gentleman Jack a brand of coffee?" he had asked her. A smile was his answer and then he began to tell her about his latest idea to acquire fame and fortune.

Wanda listened to Bo say all of the right things, the words us, we and our absorbed and embraced by her. She didn't need another cup of her favorite coffee for her to say, "I love your ideas." Her tiny eyes radiating love as she peered at Bo over her empty cup. "I just love books; all kinds of books; rare editions; leather bound books; even books on compact disks."

She set her cup gently down onto her saucer. "I don't like those new fangled electronic books," she said, her nose crinkling up. "They're too cold and impersonal. Being able to turn a real page makes me feel a part of the story and the author."

"I totally agree with you, Miss Mensch," said Bo, not liking the taste of the cappuccino that had turned cold. "Our business and, I hope you don't mind my calling it our business," he said cautiously. "Our business, as I envision it and, please share your visions with me, would serve gourmet coffees like we are enjoying now," he said, nodding at her cup. "We would have bistro table's ideal for his and her laptop computers and provide Wi-Fi connections for our patrons." His black eyes smiled at her. "I'd love it if you'd be the one to give our new business a name."

Wanda was beyond thrilled. She had never experienced such genuine sincerity, such an outpouring from the heart. Wanda Mensch was overwhelmed. She knew that another cup of Gentleman Jack would end up elevating Berthold Pepperwall into a second bronzed statue outside of her apartment above Shake's Mortuary and she wished for her leather riding crop to be in her hand.

What Bo Pepperwall was unaware of, as well as the entire population of Glen Forest on the Watercourse, except his sister, Arvia, was that Wanda Mensch had money; plenty of it. Only one thought kept going through Wanda's mind, well, actually two thoughts. She was going to share her wealth with Berthold Bo Pepperwall. That was her primary thought. The second thing on her mind was the string attached to her generosity. That came in the form of an iron clad contract that had Bo Pepperwall becoming an indentured servant to Wanda Mensch.

Wanda's contract had clauses that addressed her fantasies, erotic wardrobe and leather riding crop. Bo would follow her orders until death did he part.

"Now you promise that what I'm about to tell you will never leave this apartment," she whispered, cuddled up with Bo on an uncomfortable settee in the corner of her living room.

Bo shook his head and said, "Anything for you, dearest, Wanda."

Then Wanda Mensch opened up her computerized brain, her hi-tech filing system and told her new love how all of Mayor Bell's campaign funds from the fateful night of his death had mysteriously became hers. "Not a single, solitary soul claimed a red cent," she said to Bo. "Nothing," she whispered. She paused, blinked her eyelids several times and said, "Berthold, would you be a dear and help me manage all of that money?"

CLICK/SNAP!

The next evening surrounded by a myriad of financial statements, Bo and Wanda were once again snuggled up on the settee like two proverbial love birds. Balanced between them was a single glass of dandelion wine. They passed the glass back and forth taking sips in between discussing, among other things, their new, exciting future together. "Do you have a favorite season of the year?" he asked feeling an urge to change the subject from business and money to find out more about his new love.

"I know this will sound strange, but I love winter," she said, her voice almost a relaxed snooze.

"Interesting," he said, feeling the effects of the homemade wine that had double the alcohol content of the commercial products. "Why winter?" he asked his right knee sliding over her near thigh.

"I like snow," she said, her near shoulder pushing against his. "I was raised near a small tourist town in northern Wisconsin. It was called Minocqua; did you ever hear of it?"

"I've heard of it," said Bo, a tired smile making half an appearance. "I told Sam a story about my parents when we kind of bumped into one another the other night when I was taking out the garbage."

Wanda's thigh pressed against Bo's knee. "Did you tell Sam that Minocqua's an island, dearest Bo?" she said, her question sounding like her Mensa qualifications were greater than his. "More specifically it comes from the Ojibwe Indian name, Ninocqua, meaning noon-day rest." She paused, her knee moving up and over; searching; delicately rubbing. "The Ojibwe, at least the Lac du Flambeau band I grew up with, live in a nearby town by the same name. It's on their reservation

"Gee," said Bo, a grin appearing. "I didn't know I was in love with Pocahontas."

Wanda's knee jammed into her target. "Right love, wrong tribe," she said, spilling a drop of wine on her hand.

Bo leaned over and licked it off. "Wrong tribe, right sensuous squaw," he said, looking at her and savoring the new feeling of love he felt. "Just how come you happen to know all of this Native American stuff?" he asked.

"I told you," she said. "I was born and raised there. My parents had a small sporting goods store; sold fishing tackle and live bait. It was located west of town on Highway 70 and D. I loved it there. I had a girlfriend my age who lived across the road. Her parents owned the motel there. I think it was called The Towers. Then, one day, my mother ran off with a fishing rod salesman."

Bo could see her eyes get moist and, for the first time in his life, he made sure his brain was engaged when he said, "Well, my father ran off with some singer he met in a saloon." He continued to think. "Kind of makes us kindred spirits, doesn't' it?" He took Wanda in his arms and hugged her harder than he ever hugged anyone including his mother when she had told him she was dying. "Hey, Miss Mensch," he said tenderly stroking her mousey brown hair, "we could move up to your island town if you'd like." He stroked her hair some more. "We could still have our coffee house. We've got plenty of money. We can even buy a house with a fireplace. I heard making love by a fire is really the most romantic setting in the world." He gave her a hug.

"Is that what you really want?" she asked then standing up in front of him.

Bo nodded.

"Follow me," she ordered.

Bo found no trouble obeying her when she shouted with a slap of her riding crop across her open hand: "On your knees, Spartacus." All he could see was the amount in her checkbook balance, six figures pushing seven.

Wanda's orders had no sooner left her lips when a startled look shoved aside the one of passion that had ridden with her. "Did you hear that?" she asked, her pulsating hormones colliding with a noise outside she thought she heard.

"I did, my love," said Bo. His tilted mustache seemed to lie on an even keel. "It sounded like a horse."

In the middle of the town square, General Glen Forest Pepperwall, complete with an additional new patina of pigeon droppings, continued to brandish his saber, his steed reared back on hind legs, the high school's senior class paint job faded and awaiting next year's class. Had Wanda's tiny apartment faced the square instead of the parking lot in back of the mortuary, had she had the same view Sam, Amanda and Matilda had from their apartment facing the square, she and Bo might have been able to make out a smile on the Generals lips.

EPILOGUE

Sam couldn't have been happier. He found himself working for his wife, the new principal of Glen Forest on the Watercourse High School. He was not only a Slashing Rapier but he was also a paraprofessional library aide. It was his wife's idea. She not only could keep the school's budget in the black but she could also keep an eye on the man she married for the second time. Sam's job was the same as the one his wife once did. He even used her same stool. His taste in coffee, however, was different. Strong and black.

The daily mail had been delivered and Sam sorted through the mostly periodicals before coming in contact with a small, rectangular padded mailer with his name. He gave the padding a curious squeeze and felt his heart jump. Sam knew what was in the envelope.

He sat on the stool, an empty envelope off to his right side and the contents of the envelope in his left hand. An eerie warmth crept through his hand and up his arm and spread through his entire body. A single page note rested on the counter looking up at him, smiling.

Sam:

I knew this belonged to you the moment we talked that night when we took out and, oh yes, discussed garbage and the like. Your father must've been some kind of a dynamic human being. It's too bad you never got to know him. This good luck charm of mine can't replace him but at least you'll know that it was in his hands, the same hands that should have been holding his son. Enjoy and give it a SNAP/CLICK when you think of me.

Your brother,

Bo

Title: The Jacket

- Author: Richard Baran
- Publisher: TotalRecall Publications, Inc.
- Hard Cover ISBN: 9781590955659
- Paperback, ISBN: 9781590955666
- Ebook, Nook, Kindle, ISBN: 9781590955673
- Number of pages: 352
- Publication Date: 2013

Tidge Mackiewicz, new patriarch of his family, received several orders from his dying father, Kid Scream. One order stated that Tidge should quit believing in Santa Claus and stop acting like every day was Christmas. Tidge should also abandon his belief that the Luftwaffe shot down Santa Claus on Christmas Eve in 1944 and Santa survived.

Title: The Dutchman's Gift

- Author: Richard Baran
- Publisher: TotalRecall Publications, Inc.
- Paperback, ISBN: 9781590952979
- Ebook, Nook, Kindle, ISBN: 9781590952986
- Number of pages: 128
- Publication Date: 2015

Riley "Rocky" Stone, a twelve year old boy on a family vacation in Arizona, finds what he believes is an Apache arrowhead while hiking with his grandfather and family in Arizona's Superstition Mountains. When Riley returns to his home in Chicago after the vacation he closely examines his arrowhead. He discovers that one side has etchings of three circles—two small and one large. His grandfather had explained to him that the Native Americans communicated with crude drawings using circles and stick figures; the circles representing stages of life; a figure drawn upside down meant death. When Riley rotates his arrowhead where the two smaller circles sit atop the larger circle he sees death replaced by the image of Mickey Mouse.

Title: Where Have All the Go-Go's Gone
Book One

- Author: Richard Baran
- Publisher: TotalRecall Publications, Inc.
- Hard Cover ISBN: 9781590952399
- Paperback, ISBN: 9781590952405
- Ebook, Nook, Kindle, ISBN: 9781590952412
- Number of pages: 296
- Publication Date: 2013

Bo Pepperwall's intelligence dwarfed Mensa's parameters. He was perceived as strange thereby resulting in his being ridiculed by many, shunned by most and being called Bo the Schmoe by all. Then he faced a dilemma. He had to choose between money (which he never had) and morals (which he also lacked). Should he weasel a part of his recently widowed sister's inheritance for a business venture or should he turn in the killer of her husband, his despicable brother-in-law? He chooses both. Bo opens La Tinkerbelle's a Go-Go, a 1960's retro discotheque in an abandoned factory building in a Chicago slum using a theme from the legend of Peter Pan. Surrounding himself with bizarre employees (each having a unique vision of reality) who put fun into dysfunctional, his dream nearly goes bust. Then a Chicago gossip columnist prints a story that has customers lined up and Bo collides with his dilemma. The collision buries him in money and public adulation. Success, however, can't cover his moral guilt in the surprise ending to Book One of this screwball murder mystery farce that is more farce than mystery.

Title: When Will They Ever Learn?

Book Two

- Author: Richard Baran
- Publisher: TotalRecall Publications, Inc.
- Hard Cover ISBN: 9781590952429
- Paperback, ISBN: 9781590952436
- Ebook, Nook, Kindle, ISBN: 9781590952443
- Number of pages: 224
- Publication Date: 2015

Bo Pepperwall is a card carrying member of Mensa, dreamer, conniver and ridiculed lifelong loser. He has witnessed the murder of his despicable brother-in-law, the mayor of Glen Forest on the Watercourse, a prestigious Chicago North Shore community. While wrestling with this moral guilt, he opens *La Tinkerbelle's a Go-Go*, a 1960's retro discotheque located in a Chicago slum and uses a theme from the legend of Peter Pan that includes a scantily clad Tinker Bell. Bo, however, remains a loser and his garish disco faces bankruptcy until an article by a Chicago gossip columnist turns it into a bonanza. That same day, Tinker Bell's outraged mother accidentally sets fire to La Tinkerbelle's and destroys the booming business. Bo and his employees—along with two black cats named Heckle and Jeckle—end up in court charged with violations of the Mann Act; contributing to the delinquency of minors; ignoring EPA laws; multiple business violations; cruelty to animals and presenting lewd and indecent performances. Bo turns in the killer and the court finds him innocent of the criminal charges in the ending to Book Two of this zany murder mystery comedy.